In Love with the Amish Nanny

REBECCA KERTZ

Could caring for
this family heal her
broken heart?

LOVE INSPIRED

INSPIRATIONAL ROMANCE

Uplifting stories of faith, forgiveness and hope.

Fall in love with stories where faith helps guide you through life's challenges, and discover the promise of a new beginning.

AVAILABLE THIS MONTH

ISBN-13: 978-1-335-58512-7

IN LOVE WITH THE AMISH NANNY
REBECCA KERTZ

CLAIMING HER TEXAS FAMILY
JOLENE NAVARRO

THEIR MAKE-BELIEVE MATCH
JACKIE STEF

THE SECRET BETWEEN THEM
SUSANNE DIETZE

THE COWBOY'S JOURNEY HOME
LINDA GOODNIGHT

EMBRACING HIS PAST
CHRISTINA MILLER

LIATMIFC0722

"Katie, what's wrong?"

Katie shook her head, unwilling to confess the truth.

"Tell me," Micah urged with a look of concern.

Katie briefly held his gaze before she looked down, anywhere but at him. He was so handsome that he stole her breath every time she saw him. The ease of their conversation had only brought home to her how much she wished things were different, that he wasn't a widower who only wanted a mother for his children.

"I'm fine, Micah." Katie unwrapped the quilt and offered it to him.

His blue gaze seemed to regard her thoughtfully. "I don't need it, but *danki*."

She nodded and stood. She felt anxious suddenly, and she wished that the storm would pass so that she could be on her way home— and away from Micah.

"The storm doesn't look like it will be ending soon," he said after they'd heard another reverberating rumble of thunder.

Katie wished that *Gott* had chosen a different path for her.

One that didn't include a dead fiancé...or his older brother, who clearly had loved his wife too much to fall in love again.

Rebecca Kertz was first introduced to the Amish when her husband took a job with an Amish construction crew. She enjoyed watching the Amish foreman's children at play and swapping recipes with his wife. Rebecca resides in Delaware with her husband and dog. She has a strong faith in God and feels blessed to have family nearby. Besides writing, she enjoys reading, doing crafts and visiting Lancaster County.

Books by Rebecca Kertz

Love Inspired

Loving Her Amish Neighbor
In Love with the Amish Nanny

Women of Lancaster County

A Secret Amish Love
Her Amish Christmas Sweetheart
Her Forgiving Amish Heart
Her Amish Christmas Gift
His Suitable Amish Wife
Finding Her Amish Love

Lancaster County Weddings

Noah's Sweetheart
Jedidiah's Bride
A Wife for Jacob
Elijah and the Widow
Loving Isaac

Visit the Author Profile page at LoveInspired.com for more titles.

In Love with the Amish Nanny

Rebecca Kertz

LOVE INSPIRED
INSPIRATIONAL ROMANCE

LOVE INSPIRED®

INSPIRATIONAL ROMANCE

Recycling programs for this product may not exist in your area.

ISBN-13: 978-1-335-58512-7

In Love with the Amish Nanny

Copyright © 2022 by Rebecca Kertz

For questions and comments about the quality of this book, please contact us at CustomerService@Harlequin.com.

Love Inspired
22 Adelaide St. West, 41st Floor
Toronto, Ontario M5H 4E3, Canada
www.LoveInspired.com

Printed in U.S.A.

Whoso findeth a wife findeth a good thing,
and obtaineth favour of the Lord.
—*Proverbs* 18:22

For Colleen, with love

Chapter One

Early August, Lancaster County, Pennsylvania

She thought she saw him this morning. Again. The wagon had passed, and she caught sight of the back of his head with his straw hat tugged forward, giving her a glimpse of his light brown hair. His royal blue short-sleeved shirt stretched over his wide shoulders, and she saw the cross of his dark suspenders in the center of his back. She would have known that familiar form anywhere. Except it was impossible. Because Jacob, her betrothed, was dead. He'd died in a farming accident a month before they were to marry nearly a year ago.

Katie Mast stared down at the vegetable garden in her parents' backyard. Weeds had sprung up after the last two days of rain, and it was her job to pull them. She knelt on the edge of the garden and coaxed out the first weed near a zucchini plant. Placing it in a bucket, she tilted her head up and allowed the warm summer breeze to caress her face. The sunshine felt good, but it didn't stop her tears as she thought of the man she'd loved and lost. She'd kept herself together for months now and thought her grief was finally easing, but seeing someone who looked a lot like Jacob brought back the pain.

She continued to pull weeds, being careful not to tug on the roots of the vegetable plants, placing each plant in a bucket. Would she ever be able to fully get over her loss? Jacob had been the love of her life and now he was dead. She would never be married to him, never have a home with him. Never have his children.

She'd always wanted a husband and children, but it wasn't meant to be. She was devastated by the loss of the only man she'd ever loved, her soulmate.

She frowned. Katie knew her parents worried about her. They constantly urged to go to a youth singing to find someone new, but she couldn't do it. It didn't seem right. How could she when the memory of the day she'd learned Jacob had been run over by farm equipment while harvesting a field still made her heart ache like it had happened only yesterday?

Why? Why did he have to die? What was Jacob doing that day working alone on his family's farm field? No one in his family knew the reason. Jacob didn't like farming. He'd wanted to be a farrier, and he'd been excited to work as an apprentice under Peter Troyer, the best farrier in New Berne. Jacob should never have been working in that field alone. None of the details of his death and the time leading up to it made any sense.

It was his time to go.

He's in a better place now.

He's with Gott.

How often had she heard members of her Amish community say those words to her? None of them had brought her comfort. Katie jerked on a weed a little too aggressively, nearly uprooting a tomato plant before she pulled it from the damp soil. Breathing deeply to calm herself, she offered up a silent prayer that the Lord would give her the strength to continue her life alone. For she would never marry. She could never marry a man she didn't love, and the man she loved no longer existed on this earth.

A harsh sob burst from her throat. "Please, Lord, help me."

"Katie! *Katie!*" Her mother's call broke through the haze of grief that was starting to overwhelm her.

Katie took a moment to pull herself together, wiped her eyes with the back of her hand and turned to see her *mam*'s face briefly in the kitchen window. "*Ja*, Mam?" she called back.

"Would you please come inside? We have a guest."

"Coming!" Katie frowned. A guest? Who? She stood, glanced down and saw that the bottom edge of her dress was dirty. Not the best way to greet a visitor, but there was nothing she could do about it.

After she washed her hands at the water pump in the backyard, Katie headed toward the house. As she hurried, she prayed that her mother hadn't invited a man for her to meet. Mam had been hinting that she needed a husband, but Katie wasn't interested in meeting anyone new. She'd told her mother that. If she couldn't have Jacob, she wouldn't marry. *Ever*.

Entering the kitchen, she found her mother seated

at the table with a younger woman, who wore an Amish head covering on her dark brown hair that was different from those worn here in Lancaster County. The woman had a kind face, and Katie found herself relaxing as their visitor smiled at her.

"There you are," Mam said. "Naomi, this is my *dochter* Katie. Katie, meet Naomi Hostetler. She is visiting from Michigan."

"Hallo," Katie greeted with a small smile as she moved farther into the room.

Her mother caught sight of Katie's dress hem and frowned. *"Katie."*

Her face heating with embarrassment, Katie brushed down the length of her skirt as if she somehow could remove the thin wet soil stain. "I was gardening, Mam."

"A hard worker," the other woman said with an approving twinkle in her warm brown eyes. "It's nice to meet you, Katie."

She nodded then felt a prickle of unease as the woman and Mam exchanged secretive glances. Her mother gestured to a chair. "Have a seat."

Katie obeyed and sat down, feeling more than a little self-conscious.

"Would you like some tea?" Mam asked, starting to rise to wait on her. "The water is still hot."

She gestured to keep her mother seated. *"Ja,* I'd like a cup, but I'll get it. Would either of you like more?"

"Nay, we still have some," Mam said.

Katie made herself tea before returning to the table and taking the seat across from their visitor. "Do you have family in the area?" she asked, wondering why a woman would come all the way from Michigan to visit New Berne.

"My *schweschter* Berta lives here," Naomi said pleasantly. "I'm considering a move to the area permanently." She smiled. "I'll be staying a few months with Berta until I can decide."

Katie nodded then took a sip of tea. The warmth of the brew felt good sliding down her throat. She wondered why her mother wanted her to come inside. "Do you need someone to show you around town?" Was that why Mam asked Katie in to meet the woman?

Naomi shook her head. "I came to talk with you."

She frowned. "You did?"

"*Ja*, I have someone I'd like you to meet. A widower with three children."

"Excuse me?"

"Naomi is a matchmaker, *dochter,*" her mother said.

Katie jumped up from her seat. "I don't want to be matched!" she cried, her eyes suddenly filling with tears. "You know that."

"Sit down, Katie." Her mother's voice was gentle, but firm. "There will be no forcing you to do anything you don't want to do."

Relieved, Katie sat back down, her intertwined fingers clenched tightly on the table. "I'm sorry, but I—"

Naomi placed her hand over Katie's. "I understand what you've been through. It's a terrible thing. I don't blame you for not wanting to move on with your life. It's hard without the man you love, *ja*?"

Katie nodded, her tears overflowing. She quickly wiped them away.

"But what are you going to do without a husband and family?" the woman asked softly. "You have to be practical. How will you provide for yourself in the coming years?"

Katie had already thought about this. "I can sew well. I plan to support myself as a seamstress."

"Commendable," Naomi said with compassion in her gaze. "Will you live with your parents forever?"

Katie blinked. "*Nay.* I'll find a place of my own."

"Will you be able to afford to live on your own with the money you make as a seamstress?"

"I think so. I'll work for Englishers as well as anyone who needs my services in our community," she said. But Katie wondered if she could do it. *I have to.* There was no other choice for her since she would be living the rest of her life as a spinster.

"May I make a suggestion?" Naomi asked as she absently stirred the tea in her cup with a spoon.

Eyeing her warily, Katie nodded and gripped her teacup.

"The widower? He is a man who has suffered a great loss. His three children are young, and he recently moved to the area to get help from his family. He finds it hard to work to support his children when he has no one to babysit them. His mother is watching his children. Unfortunately, Micah's parents also have his younger siblings to care for at home. His father works long hours away from the farm, which leaves his *mam* to handle everything at home. They love and want to help their *soohn*, which is why he asked me to find him a wife."

Katie listened and couldn't help feeling sad for the

man who had lost his wife and the mother of his children. "I'm sorry for his loss, but I don't plan to wed. Ever."

"Why?" Naomi asked. "There are different types of marriage within our communities and not all are love matches. There are unions of two people who are deeply in love, and there are marriages born of two people who become companions to help each other because circumstances make it better for them to be together rather than alone." She watched Katie carefully as she sipped from her tea. "Will you at least meet him? If nothing else, if you are comfortable doing so, you can offer to watch his children while he works. Temporarily until he remarries."

Katie's gaze went to her mother, who appeared worried. *About me*, she realized. She'd caused her parents nothing but worry since learning of Jacob's fatal accident. She wanted to ease her mother's concern, and if she could help the man who needed a babysitter while simultaneously lessening her parents' burden, she'd do it. She'd offer to watch this Micah's children for him.

"If I meet with him and it suits us both that I babysit his *kinner*, will you continue to look for a wife for him? That's what he wants, *ja*?"

"Ja," Naomi said. "He needs one. I'm not sure if he has a choice of not marrying again."

"Mam?" Katie wanted her mother's advice.

"It's up to you, Katie, but I think watching his little ones if nothing else will be *gut* for you. You always wanted a family of your own. Helping Micah will allow you to spend time with *kinner* who don't have a *mudder*, especially since you don't plan to have any of your own."

Blinking rapidly against tears, she could only nod. "Sometimes *Gott* has other plans for us," Katie said. "But I will meet him and watch his children if he is agreeable."

"Gut." Naomi finished her tea and stood. "Can you be ready to meet him tomorrow afternoon? Say at two? I'll double-check with him and get back with you if there is a change."

Feeling a sudden attack of nerves, Katie hesitated.

"It will be *oll recht*, Katie," Naomi assured her. "He is a *gut* man. I know that you understand the pain of his loss. He'll appreciate that you want to help in his time of need."

Katie nodded. "I can be ready at two."

"Gut. If you don't hear from me again today, then expect me tomorrow. It's best if I take you so that I can introduce you to each other," the woman said.

Standing in his side yard, Micah Bontrager gazed with satisfaction at the house he was renovating. Soon to be his new home for him and his children. Although he had a lot of work left inside, he was pleased with how much he'd accomplished today in the kitchen. Fortunately, the man who'd sold him the property had replaced the roof and siding before he'd put the house on the market. The farmhouse had come with eighty acres of rich farmland. Fixing the interior of the residence was necessary first, as it was too late in the season for planting anything new. However, there were ten acres of hay already planted by the previous owner, ensuring Micah would be harvesting hay before the end of September. By late October he'd be picking fruit from the five fall apple trees on his property not far from the house.

Micah climbed into his market wagon and headed home to his parents' farm. It was a sunny day in August, and the warm breeze filtering in through the open side windows of his buggy felt good on his face. He thought about how much his life had changed in the past year. After his beloved wife Anna's passing, he'd found it difficult to work and care for his three children at their home in Michigan. Members of his community there had helped him with childcare, but he'd felt it wasn't right for him to keep accepting their aid. With Anna gone and none of her family—or his—in the area, there had been no reason for him to stay in Centreville. And he'd thought his parents deserved the opportunity to spend time with their grandchildren, with the distance between Michigan and Pennsylvania making it difficult for him to see his family. He missed his father, mother and siblings, and he knew they would pitch in when he needed them until he could make other arrangements for his children's care. So, he'd sold his property in Centreville, Michigan, and moved his young family to New Berne in Lancaster County, Pennsylvania, where his parents had moved two years previously.

Micah was grateful for his family's love and support. His heart hurt from his loss of Anna, and although he didn't want to marry again, he realized he had to for his children's sake. Jacob, Rebecca and Eliza needed a mother. He couldn't be both mother and father to them while working to support them. He needed someone to take care of his children and make his house a home while he provided for them. So, he'd asked a matchmaker, Naomi Hostetler back in Michigan, to help him find a wife. She'd been the one who had introduced him to Anna, and it hadn't taken long for the love between them to grow into something special. To his surprise, when he'd moved away, Naomi had followed. Naomi had told him that she had a sister in New Berne she'd been wanting to visit and she could continue her search for his wife there. The thought of another woman in his life, another wife, upset him, but the choice had been stolen from him the moment Anna had died from double pneumonia, a complication after contracting the flu. He'd no idea that Anna had suffered from asthma as a child—or that asthma never went away as an adult, although she'd seemed fine when they'd met and after they'd married. He needed a spouse but he didn't want love. He'd loved and lost Anna, and he didn't want to suffer another loss.

Another few weeks of work and the house would be livable, he thought as he drove down the road toward his parents' farm. Today he'd replaced the kitchen floor and installed wall cabinets. Tomorrow he'd install the base cabinets and the countertop. Fortunately, he'd made enough from the sale of his farm in Centreville to finance the trip and the farm property here in New Berne with enough money left over for renovations and other expenses. Micah had known the trip from Centreville to New Berne would take nearly ten hours by car. He couldn't drive a buggy that great distance, and the cost of having his moved was too much considering the age of the vehicle. So, before he'd left, he had sold his family buggy and had purchased a used one in excellent condition within a day of arriving in New Berne. The carriage was a lot like the one he'd had in Michigan, but the color was gray instead of black. It was a formerly owned buggy in great shape and still a long while from having to be rebuilt for continued use. It was in much better condition than his old one. And it was big enough for a growing family. It was possible that after he remarried, his new wife would want more children. Micah closed his eyes as he reminded himself that taking a second spouse was necessary because he needed a mother for his children. Although it wouldn't be a love match, he wouldn't deny her if she wanted to give birth.

Micah pulled onto his father's property and parked near the barn. He sat a minute, willing to admit that he felt bad for bringing his family to his parents' door. While his mother was happy to have her grandchildren close, he knew it was still a burden for him to be here. He thought of his middle brother. Anna had been sick at the time of his death and he'd been unable to leave and attend his brother's funeral. Anna's death occurred within a week of his sibling's. Afterward, Micah should have gone home to check on his family, but the deep pain of his loss and his struggles to manage without his wife had made traveling impossible.

After inhaling then releasing a deep breath, Micah climbed down from the wagon he'd borrowed from his father, pulled by one of the horses he'd had trailered in from Michigan. A buggy entered the yard as he started toward the house. He paused as the vehicle pulled up next to him and stopped. He immediately recognized Naomi Hostetler in the driver's seat. His stomach felt as if suddenly filled with lead. He'd hired the matchmaker because he'd had to. At least his parents had thought it a good idea at the time they'd met her. They'd managed to convince him after he'd moved to New Berne to allow Naomi to continue to find a match for him.

"Micah," the woman greeted through the open window. "Just the man I'd wanted to see."

"Ja?" He moved closer to the vehicle, his stomach churning.

"I've got news for you."

Everything in him wanted to pull back from remarrying. "Naomi…"

"Now, Micah, you need a wife. You know it's best for the little ones."

He swallowed hard and nodded, as visions of his sick wife filled his mind, compounded with the guilt of being forced to move on. "Will you come inside?"

The matchmaker grinned. *"Ja,* I'll be right in."

Micah headed toward the house. He entered the kitchen, took off his hat and hung it on a wall hook. His mother was at the stove, putting the kettle on.

"Soohn, did you have a *gut* day?" she asked, turning to face him with a smile.

"Ja, I got the floor done in the kitchen."

Mam looked pleased. "The heart of a home. Good choice to finish that room first, Micah."

Micah shifted uncomfortably. "Naomi Hostetler is here."

"Is she now?" She smirked.

He nodded. "*Ja*, said that she has news for me."

His mother approached him, placed a gentle hand on his arm. "I know it isn't easy."

"*Nay*, it's not." He saw a batch of cookies cooling on the kitchen counter. "Where are my little ones?"

"Your eldest, Jacob, is upstairs playing with Emma." Mam untied her quilted apron and removed it from around her waist. "Your two *bubbel* are napping. Your *schweschter* is *wunderbor* at keeping children entertained. They are *gut kinner, soohn*."

"It was their *mudder*'s influence."

His *mam* shook her head. "*Nay*, she has been gone ten months now. You've had a hand in how well-behaved they are."

Micah glanced away, unwilling to take credit for his children's good behavior.

"I should get washed up before Naomi settles in to talk with us." He went toward the bathroom at the back of the house and washed his hands and then his face. After drying himself, he reentered the kitchen and found the matchmaker seated at the kitchen table with his mother, drinking tea.

"Micah," Naomi greeted with a smile. "Join us."

He approached, his heart beating wildly. How could he marry another after losing the love of his life? Micah took the seat at the end of the table between the two women. There was a cup of coffee instead of tea waiting for him, fixed just the way he liked it. He cracked a smile for the woman who'd raised him. "You have some news?" he said to Naomi.

"Ja." The matchmaker nodded. "There is a young woman who has agreed to meet you."

Micah raised an eyebrow. Naomi knew, though, that he wanted a wife not a love match. "How old is she?"

"Twenty-one." A flicker of concern crossed Naomi's face. "She lost the man she loved a month before they were to be married."

"So young," he murmured, sympathetic. "I'm sorry to hear that."

"I have to tell you, Micah, that she doesn't want to marry. *Ever.* Her parents worry about her, and they wish nothing more than to see her with a husband and children, but she has had a difficult time. She has agreed to meet you so that she can help you with your *kinner.* I don't know if anything will come of your meeting except that you may have a potential temporary babysitter."

"She doesn't ever want to marry?" He frowned. "Why do I need her help?"

"Because your parents have enough on their plate, and Katie will handle your three well. She loves *kinner."*

He wasn't sure what to say. She'd suffered a loss like he had. He hated the thought that a twenty-one-year-old had endured such awful pain. "It would be nice to have someone help me with them," he admitted. "Mam and Dat have enough to do."

Naomi nodded. "Exactly." She sighed. "It's a shame. Katie is meant to be a wife and *mudder* even if she doesn't believe it. It's possible she will change her mind, but I doubt it."

"Katie," he murmured thoughtfully.

"Katie Mast."

His gaze went to his mother. "Do you know this young woman?"

Mam's expression was grave as she nodded. "What happened to her was tragic. She is a lovely young woman who deserves to be happy." To his surprise, he saw tears fill his mother's eyes.

"I would like to meet her," he said. A grieving single woman should not be forced to wed, he thought. Still, if it suited her, he could use her aid. Maybe they could help each other. "When?"

Naomi sat up straighter in her seat. "I thought I'd bring her by your *haus* tomorrow. I hear you've been working hard to make it a home for you and your *kinner*."

"What time?" he asked after a nod.

"About two?" The matchmaker watched him closely, making him suddenly aware of her intense scrutiny. "I'll continue to look for a wife for you, Micah. In the meantime, you'll find Katie a big help with your children."

Micah nodded. "I'll be ready to meet her tomorrow at the *haus* at two." At least, he hoped he'd be ready. He wasn't eager to have any new woman in his life, even one who would be watching his children temporarily.

Chapter Two

Katie washed up after a morning of baking. She dressed carefully in her light blue dress, white cape with apron and a white prayer *kapp* pinned to her rolled blond hair.

She was nervous about meeting Micah regarding his children and she had no idea why. It wasn't like she'd agreed to marry him.

"Katie!" her mother called from downstairs. "Naomi's here."

"I'll be right there!" Drawing a calming breath, Katie ran a hand over her head covering to make sure it and her hair were still neatly in place.

Vanity was a sin, but that wasn't why she fussed over her appearance. She wanted to make sure that the man, Micah, liked what he saw so he would trust her. The prospect of spending time with children other than her own younger siblings excited her. Maybe he would even allow her to mend or make the children's clothes. She would do it for the cost of the fabric and nothing more. A good way to hone her sewing skills and have others see what she could do for them so that word would spread about her services as a seamstress.

A funny flutter stirred in her belly as Katie slowly descended the stairs. Naomi greeted her with a smile when she entered the kitchen.

"Are you ready to go?" the woman asked.

Katie nodded and grabbed the pound cake she'd made for Micah to make a good impression, before she turned toward her mother. "Mam, I don't know if I should do this."

"Why not?" Naomi's expression filled with compassion. "You're planning to babysit not marry him, *ja*?"

"Ja," Katie admitted softly.

"Then why are you worried?"

"I guess I shouldn't be." Katie followed Naomi out to the woman's vehicle, a boxy gray buggy like the others used in Lancaster County. She climbed into the passenger side and watched Naomi get comfortable. "What can you tell me about... Micah, is it?"

"Ja. Micah. He's a kind man and *gut vadder*, but he suffered a terrible blow after his wife died while battling the flu. With the help of his community in Centreville—that's the community in Michigan where I'm from, in case you're wondering—Micah managed to work and take care of his *soohn* and two *dechter*, but he missed his family and wanted them to be able to spend time with his *kinner*. He moved here to be closer to his parents and siblings who have been living in Lancaster County for the last two years."

"I'm sorry to hear of his wife's death."

"Ja, it was sad thing, and to be truthful, I don't think

he is done grieving for her. It's hard to tell with him. He seems strong, but no one knows how he is when alone after such a loss. Micah is *gut* at hiding his feelings."

"I understand grief."

"*Ach ja.* You know what it's like, don't you, Katie?"

"I know what it's like to lose someone you love beyond any other. But we never got to marry or have children." A sudden thought startled her. "I think it is worse for Micah."

"That's kind of you to say, but loss is loss no matter the circumstances. Both are unbearable for those suffering from it."

Katie blinked back tears. *"Ja."*

About fifteen minutes after they'd left her father's property, Naomi rolled her buggy into the barnyard where a house had been built far enough from the road to have a measure of privacy. Katie glanced up at the large farmhouse and thought it had been built in mind for a family with several children. "It looks nice," she said.

Naomi smiled at her before she opened her door and climbed down. Katie followed suit and joined the matchmaker on the walkway leading up to a back door.

"The roof and siding were new when Micah bought it. The last owners never finished fixing the inside. Micah is in the middle of renovating."

Katie gazed up at the house, picturing what it might have been like for her and Jacob to share such a home if he'd lived and they'd married.

The back screen door was open. "Micah! It's Naomi."

"It's two o'clock already?" a deep voice called back, rumbling pleasantly in Katie's ears. "Come in."

The door squeaked as she followed Naomi inside. "I'll just be a minute," the man said.

The interior of the house was dark compared to the bright sunshine outside. It took a moment for Katie's eyes to adjust and for her to realize that they were in the fellow's kitchen. His back was to them as he set a piece of countertop on the base cabinets that formed an L shape. Katie might have considered it fancy but she realized that the larger cabinet and counter space would be necessary for a man with a growing family.

Katie's gaze took in the rest of the room before it returned to take in the man as he worked. She froze as she studied the back of his head and the breadth of his shoulders. The back of him looked familiar. Then Micah turned, and she reeled in shock when she locked gazes with him. "Jacob?" she whispered, feeling as if she'd spiraled back in time. She suddenly felt woozy and struggled to grab hold of the edge of the doorway to keep from falling. The pound cake she held threatened to topple onto the floor.

The man hurried to her side, and she felt the warm, firm grip of his fingers on her arm. While still holding on to her, he used his free hand to rescue the cake and set it carefully on the kitchen counter. "Is she ill?" Katie heard him ask Naomi.

"*Nay*, she's surprised, because she was startled by your appearance."

Frown lines appeared on his brow. "I don't understand."

Katie blinked rapidly as the fogginess passed.

"I'm sorry," she whispered, fighting tears. "You look so much like…"

Ignoring her apology, he continued to watch her intently, gentling the hand that held on to her arm. "Naomi?"

"She expected to meet you, but…" Naomi's voice trailed off. "Micah, this is Katie Mast."

"I'm fine," Katie said as she straightened, pulling away from him, determined to prove that she was more than fine.

"Katie, this is Micah Bontrager," Naomi said as Micah released his hold.

"Bontrager," Katie murmured. Micah must be Jacob's brother, which explained why he looked like her deceased betrothed. He and Jacob shared similar facial features and build and the same shade of light brown hair. Micah was clearly older with tiny lines at the outer corners of eyes that were a brighter shade of blue than Jacob's. The soft brown beard that outlined his outer jaw from ear to ear, leaving the rest of his handsome face shaven in the Amish way, proclaimed him as having married.

Katie released a shuddering breath and said a name no one had mentioned since his death. "Jacob's older *bruder*?"

Micah stiffened. "You knew my *bruder*?"

"Katie was betrothed to him when he died," Naomi said.

She heard Micah draw a sharp breath. He saw his pain mirrored in her pretty blue eyes. "I'm sorry," he told her. "I didn't know. My wife… I couldn't come back for his funeral."

Her heart ached, making it difficult for her to gaze at him, but Katie didn't—couldn't—look away. Her pain changed suddenly into anger. She glared at Naomi. "What is this? You knew about my relationship with his *bruder*! How could you do this? You set me up!" She turned her ire on Micah. "I don't know what to say!"

"I didn't know!" he breathed, shock in his blue eyes.

Katie closed her eyes and breathed to calm herself. Micah Bontrager had lost someone he loved like she had. And he too suffered from the loss of Jacob, his brother. It wasn't his fault that they had been forced to meet this way. He'd been set up, too. By whom? Did Naomi or her parents have something to do with this? She shook her head and stared at him. "I don't understand. Why didn't he ever mention you?" She'd known he had an older brother who'd stayed in Michigan. Naomi was visiting from Michigan. She bit her lip as she studied him. "Wait! Are you M.T.?"

He looked devastated by the turn of events. He nodded. "A nickname. No one uses it anymore." His expression turned hard as he glared at Naomi. "Did my *eldra* put you up to this?" His jaw was tight as he mentioned his parents.

Naomi shook her head. "I heard about Katie from a woman I met in Kings General Store. I didn't know Katie was the girl who was going to marry him. I only found out yesterday while talking with her *mudder*. Since Katie is just offering to watch your *kinner*, I thought meeting each other might be *gut* for the both of you." She looked shaken by their reactions as she glanced back and forth from Katie to Micah. "I wasn't trying to hurt either one of you."

Firmly in control again, Katie nodded. "I did offer to babysit," she admitted grudgingly. "I still am. I was just—"

"Startled," Micah said, his eyes softening.

"Ja." Katie recovered enough to pick up the cake she'd baked for Micah and give it to him. "I made this for you. I hope you like pound cake."

His continued scrutiny of her was unsettling, as he looked so much like Jacob it was uncanny. "I do. *Danki.*" He accepted the cake and moved it to the corner of the countertop he'd just installed where the two base cabinets met.

Katie couldn't take her gaze off him. Now that she could see him more clearly, she realized that he was more muscular than her late twenty-one-year-old fiancé. And she noticed other differences about him. His hair was a lighter shade of brown than Jacob's was, and his eyes were bigger, the lashes much thicker than his deceased brother's.

How old is Micah? Jacob had talked about having family out of state come for their wedding, but he never elaborated on any of them. She and Jacob had known each other less than a year, but it was love at first sight for her—and it seemed so for him too since he'd asked her to marry him within six months of courting her.

With a wide-eyed look, Micah searched the kitchen, his brow furrowing. "I've been so intent on the work that I didn't think to bring chairs."

"That's *oll recht*," Katie murmured shyly. "We don't have to sit. We won't be staying long, as I don't want to keep you from your day."

* * *

Micah couldn't get over the fact that Katie Mast was the woman his brother Jacob was to marry. She was a beautiful young woman with blue eyes and golden blond hair. Her light blue dress highlighted the color of her eyes, making them bluer and brighter. Her nose was slightly red from the sun, telling him that she frequently spent time outdoors. "Do you garden?" he asked suddenly.

Katie blinked. "*Ja.* Why do you ask?"

He shook his head. "It looks like you've spent time outside."

Looking horrified, she glanced down as if to check her clothing.

"It's on your nose and a bit of your cheeks, Katie," he said. When she met his gaze, he smiled. "Sunburn."

"Ach." She blushed, further brightening her cheeks.

"Naomi said that you'd be willing to watch my children while I'm at work," he observed.

Her expression softening, Katie nodded. "*Ja,* I love children, but..." She paused, her expression sad. "*Ja,* I'd be happy to watch them for you until..." Her features burned hotter, causing red from her neck up.

He glanced at Naomi, saw approval in her gaze. He would have to talk with the matchmaker later. "Can you come to my parents' *haus* to meet my *kinner*? I have three—two girls and a boy."

"How old are they?"

"My *soohn*, Jacob, is my oldest at three, nearly four, years old. My *dochter* Rebecca is two. My youngest, Eliza, is almost a year old." He studied her, noting the way her expression changed when he mentioned his son's name. He had named Jacob after his younger brother, one of the nicest people he'd ever known. He saw the way her eyes softened as he told her about his children. He'd known that Jacob was to get married, but with harvesting to be done and then Anna's sudden illness, by necessity all their plans had shifted. He'd been thrown into a tizzy and barely able to recall the names of his offspring, never mind what was happening in New Berne. Then he'd learned Jacob had died and shortly afterward Anna was gone. He'd become exhausted and unable to think straight. The men in his Centreville community had stepped in to help with the harvest while the women had pitched in with his children. Weeks turned into months until he realized something had to change. That was when he'd decided to start somewhere new where there was family, and he'd moved to New Berne.

To his delight, Katie had cracked a smile as he'd told her about his son and daughters. "I see why you might need help with three of them." She bit her lip. "Will you want me to watch them at Evan and Betty's?"

Of course, she would know his parents, he realized. "*Nay*, my *eldra* will watch them until I move us into this house. The rooms still need a bit of work, but I should be finished in three weeks."

"I'll start in three weeks then, if you want me to."

Micah nodded. "I do." He saw Katie taking stock of her surroundings.

"It's a *wunderbor* kitchen," she said, looking impressed. "I assume I'll be cooking for you and your *kinner*?"

"You want to cook for us?"

Katie inclined her head. "I love to cook and bake."

His gaze went to the pound cake on the countertop. "I'd appreciate that." He hesitated. "I can pay you."

She gasped as if insulted. "*Nay*, I could never take your money. Let me help you, *ja*? I have the time to babysit. You're a Bontrager. You're like family."

"*Danki*," he murmured, unable to take his eyes off her flawless complexion and pretty face.

"Naomi said that you'll be marrying again soon."

He frowned as he nodded. "My *kinner* need a *mudder*."

"I'll watch your little ones until you take a wife." Katie shifted her attention to the matchmaker. "I should get home," she told her.

Naomi nodded. "*Ja*. It's getting late, and I know you like to help your *mam* with supper."

Katie started toward the door, pausing once to glance back at him. "Will you send word when you want me to come?" she asked him.

"*Ja*, I'll let you know."

"*Gut*. Please give my regards to your family."

"I will." Micah watched her open the screen door and exit the house. Something about Katie Mast tugged at something deep inside him. *Because she is the woman my* bruder *loved.*

"Don't worry, Micah," Naomi said. She had stayed behind after Katie had gone outside. "You'll have your wife. I'll find a *gut* match for you. Just like you want." She peered through the screened door as Katie climbed into the matchmaker's buggy and settled in for the ride.

"Naomi—"

"I'll not force you to wed someone you don't want, Micah."

Micah looked at her without a word. Still, he gave her a nod. He didn't want to marry anyone but he had to, so what the matchmaker said seemed pointless. "Would you tell Katie to stop by the house in the morning so that she can meet my *kinner*," he said as Naomi headed toward to the door. "We didn't set a time."

"I will. Is nine okay?"

"Ja." He followed her toward the door. "Katie seems nice."

The matchmaker halted and faced him. "She is a lovely young woman who believes she'll never be happy again. I think watching your *kinner* for you while I search for your new wife will be *gut* for her."

Micah watched Naomi as she crossed the yard and climbed into the driver's seat of her vehicle. He'd never imagined that the woman willing to watch his children was the woman Jacob had loved and planned to wed. She was only twenty-one. She'd barely lived, and she was so heartbroken over his brother's death that she decided she'd never marry or have a family of her own.

"What a tragic loss," Micah murmured as the buggy pulled away and he turned back to the work at hand. He was twenty-six, and he'd been fortunate enough to have had five years with Anna before the

Lord had called her home. His throat tightened as he thought of his late spouse. She'd been a beautiful soul and a wonderful wife and mother.

Forcing away the pain, he concentrated instead on finishing the home for himself and his children…and wondering about his new wife, whoever she might eventually be.

Riding silently home in Naomi's buggy, Katie thought about meeting the widower. Her parents and his apparently had had nothing to do with the matchmaker's decision to bring them together. Coincidence? She didn't know. The fact that Micah was Jacob's older brother made her wonder what plan *Gott* had for putting them in each other's path.

Naomi shifted on the bench seat beside her. "Katie, do you have any questions now that you've met Micah?"

"Jacob mentioned an older *bruder*, M.T., who lived out of state. I had no idea his name was actually Micah."

"And now you know," Naomi said with a small smile in her direction.

"Ja." She stared out the open side window, watching the passing scenery. It was early August and corn grew in farm fields, the tall stalks green against the azure blue backdrop of the sky. The warmth of summer blew in through the window, but still she felt a chill from deep inside. "Do Evan and Betty know about my offer to watch their *kinskinner*?"

"Ach ja. They know." The matchmaker's voice was soft. "They love you and they love their *soohn.* They

know you will take *gut* care of the *kinner*." Naomi paused briefly to glance her way. "They want both of you to be happy."

"Did they set us up?"

"*Nay*, I told the truth," Naomi said. "Although I only learned about the connection between your families after I spoke with your *mam*, and then it didn't seem to matter since you only offered to babysit."

Katie rolled those words around in her mind. "I... am I doing the right thing?"

"You don't think it's a *gut* idea to help a young father in need?"

"*Nay*, it's not that."

"Then what?" Naomi turned to stare at her briefly before turning her attention back on the road. Her expression was tense, as if filled with disappointment.

"I...he looks so much like Jacob. When I saw him, it seemed as if he were Jacob years from now."

"Micah is nothing like him, Katie," the woman said. "He can't be. His life took a different path than his family. He experienced things that his younger *bruder* never did."

"I know that, but their similar looks startled me. Do you know I thought I'd seen Jacob a few times around town during the past week? I was alarmed. I believed I was finally getting over losing him until I imagined him as I went out to get the mail after he'd driven by in his wagon. But it wasn't Jacob. It must have been Micah. He and Micah look so much alike that it...hurts." When Naomi didn't say anything, Katie went on. "He could have been my *schwager*." She could tell by the matchmaker's expression that she understood that under other circumstances Micah would have been her brother-in-law.

Katie recalled the man's thick arms. "Micah seems to know what he's doing with the *haus*. He must work in construction." Whatever he did, it certainly had to involve using muscle.

"Micah is a farmer."

"What?" Katie stiffened. Jacob had died while working on his parents' farm. Why would Micah farm when farming had killed his brother?

Naomi sighed. "Katie, Micah is an experienced farmer. He's been farming all his life. He owned a farm in Centreville, where he and his *frau* settled. The land he'd lived and worked on in Michigan was vaster than the eighty acres he purchased here in New Berne. He knows what he is doing."

Katie felt a tightness in her chest. "Does he have help working the land?"

"I'm sure his *bruders* will help him."

Her fear eased a bit. His brothers Matt, Jonathan and Vernon were now old enough to help their father, Evan, with farming. Perhaps Evan would pitch in before or after his own farm work was done. "*Ja*, you're right. He has three *bruders* to help him." And three sisters, she thought, smiling as she recalled Emma, Sarie and Adel, the Bontrager sisters between the ages of twelve and fifteen with Emma the eldest at fifteen.

"Have you seen Evan and Betty lately?" Naomi asked.

"Last Sunday after church. I see them every church Sunday and occasionally on Visiting Days, but I haven't spent much time with them." Which pained her and made her feel bad that she hadn't visited with them sooner. She loved her one-time future in-laws, but after losing Jacob it had hurt too much to spend the day with them, as they were a reminder of Jacob, whom they'd loved.

"I think you should visit them," the matchmaker said. "You can do it tomorrow. Micah asked if you would stop by in the morning at nine to meet the *kinner*. I'm sure Betty if not Evan will be there."

Katie closed her eyes. Naomi was right about visiting Betty and Evan, but with the past distance between them, it wouldn't make the time at their house any easier. *It's been almost ten months since Jacob has passed. I should be able to see and visit his family without feeling awful or sad.*

"What are they expecting between Micah and me?" Katie asked quietly.

"They want for you to be more than a babysitter for their grandchildren, Katie. But don't let that stop you from helping Micah. They just want Micah to be happy. Once I find him a wife, their expectations will go away in the joy of seeing him married again with a *mudder* for his *kinner*."

Katie knew she should take comfort from Naomi's words but she didn't. Her thoughts filled with Micah and another woman, and she experienced a painful pang near her heart. *Because he looks like Jacob.*

Chapter Three

After being awake for most of the night worrying about his children's first meeting with Katie, Micah woke up before the crack of dawn to help his brothers with the farm animals while his son and daughters still slept.

He noticed some new animals in the barn, ones that hadn't been there yesterday. "Dat starting a dairy farm? Looks like he bought a few new cows."

Vernon grinned. "He's thinking about it. It was my idea."

Micah arched his eyebrow. "You?"

Matt chuckled. "*Ja*, he's got cows on the brain."

Snorting, Vern filled a water trough. "And you don't like fresh milk?"

"You can get milk from a goat, too, *bruder*," Matt said with a snort, "but you don't see me asking our *dat* to buy more goats."

"Because they chew everything in sight!" Vern exclaimed. "We've got more than enough of the critters."

Micah shook his head as he regarded his younger brothers with exasperation tempered with affection.

"Seems as if nothing's changed much around here. You two still argue about every little thing."

"Nay," the two brothers said together and then burst out laughing before they grinned at each other.

Their brother, Jonathan, entered the barn as the three of them were getting ready to leave.

"Nothing like coming early for a little work," Matt said sarcastically.

"I was helping Dat with Joe," Jonathan said.

Joe was one of the two horses the family relied on to pull their vehicles. "What's wrong with Joe?" Micah asked with concern.

"Dat said he's been limping a bit," Jonathan said. "I took a look at his rear right hoof, and I think he's suffering from a stone bruise." He rubbed his forehead. "Thought I'd ask Peter to come by and confirm it. Joe will have to settle in the barn for a time so he can recover if it is a bruise." Jonathan was apprenticing under Peter Troyer, a farrier with a solid reputation in New Berne.

Micah had learned that Jacob was working under Peter before he'd died, which made him wonder, now and again, why Jacob had decided to get a jump on harvesting when no one else was around to help. He had complete faith in Jonathan's diagnosis. "Dat can use one of my horses while Joe heals."

Hungry and wondering if his children were up yet, Micah returned to the house with his brothers for breakfast. His mother had the table set, and he inhaled with gratitude the smell of coffee mingled with the scent of freshly baked muffins.

"Why didn't you tell me Katie and Jacob were to

be married?" Micah asked his mother after he and his brothers were seated at the table. He brought his coffee cup to his lips and sipped, enjoying the taste of brew.

Mam pulled a fresh tin of muffins out of the oven and set them on a hot mat on the counter. Sorrow filled her expression as she faced him. "I didn't know at first who Naomi had in mind for you. Once I found out, I didn't want you to make the connection between her and us ahead of time. I thought it best if you met her without prejudice."

"Katie is great," his young brother Matt said. "But ever since…" He looked away, unable to continue.

"How did you meet Katie?" Jonathan asked.

"The matchmaker introduced him," Vernon said.

Matt blinked. "Wait. *What?* Katie is your match?"

"Nay," Micah assured them. "She offered to help with my *kinner* until I can marry again."

Jonathan reached for a muffin from the plate at his end of the table. "Katie would make a *gut* wife."

"She's still grieving." Vernon got up and poured himself another cup of coffee from the pot on the stove. He faced them, leaning back against the counter. "Which is why she hasn't been around us since the funeral."

Micah felt terrible. "Why was Jacob working the farm alone?" His gaze settled on each brother, who appeared stricken.

"We don't know why," Jonathan said. "He never liked farming, but he knew how to farm. The work didn't need to be done immediately."

"Vernon and I were working on a construction job site," Matt said, staring down at his plate.

"Your *mudder* and I had gone into town for supplies," their *dat* said as he entered the room.

Mam gazed at each of her boys. "I don't know if we'll ever know or understand what happened."

His sister Emma entered the room. "I heard what you've been saying." She took a seat at the table and poured herself a glass of orange juice. "I think there was something wrong with him."

Micah narrowed his eyes. "What do you mean?"

Emma met his gaze. "I…he seemed off, like he wasn't feeling well."

"Why didn't he tell any of us?" Mam asked, upset.

"I asked him if he was *oll recht*, and he said he was fine." Jonathan handed her the plate of muffins, and Emma took one filled with chocolate chips.

"Was he unhappy?" Dat asked. "With the wedding the next month and his recent apprenticeship with Peter?" He took a seat at the table and grabbed for a muffin. He smiled at Mam when she handed him a cup of coffee.

"Nay," Emma said, spreading butter over her muffin. "He was happy to marry Katie." She set down her knife and looked at their father. "He liked working with Pete, too. I think it was something else that worried him." She took a bite of her muffin, chewed then swallowed. "I saw him sway and grab the doorframe to keep himself steady. When I asked him about it, he just grinned and said he hadn't slept well and was tired. I believed him." She looked upset that she had.

Watching his sister, Micah thought about what she'd told him. Jacob always had been the one person with the ever-present smile. It didn't surprise him to learn that he might not have been feeling well when he decided to start harvesting one of the back fields on their father's land.

The family got quiet for a minute as they continued to eat breakfast. Micah's youngest sisters Sarie and Adel entered the room. Sarie held Micah's baby daughter Eliza while Addie carried his middle child, Rebecca. His son Jacob walked closely beside Addie, holding on to the back of her skirt.

Young Jacob saw him. "Dat," he greeted with a sloppy smile as he moved up to him.

Micah's heart melted as it usually did whenever he saw children. "You're awake. Are you hungry?" His son bobbed his head. Micah turned to smile at his sisters. "*Gut* morning. Thanks for getting them up and dressed."

Sarie beamed at him and set Eliza into a high chair. "I enjoy your little ones." She stood back, held his gaze. "I'm glad you moved here, Micah," she said softly.

Addie sat down with Rebecca in her lap. "*Hallo*, everyone," his sister said, holding Rebecca easily as she reached for a muffin and broke it into bite-size pieces. She gave a piece to Rebecca who chewed and swallowed.

Matt finished his breakfast and stood. "Time to go, Vernon," he said. "We've got a lot to do on the job site today."

Micah nodded. Matt and Vernon worked for a local construction company when they weren't helping at the farm.

The brothers grabbed their hats and started out the door. Matt stilled then turned toward Micah. "Katie's here," he said.

Soon, the family was scrambling to give Micah and

his offspring privacy so that the children could meet Katie for the first time alone. His father moved to leave.

"Dat, take one of my horses until Joe recovers," he said.

"Danki, soohn," he said before he escaped into another room of the house. Addie, Sarie and Emma fled the room with the intention of cleaning the upstairs bedrooms.

He spoke to his mother before she could exit. "Mam, stay," Micah said gently. "When was the last time you spent any time with Katie?"

"Months ago," his mother said with a sad smile. "She hasn't visited since…"

Since his brother Jacob's death. Micah squeezed his *mam's* shoulder. "Then stay a moment, at least, to say *hallo.*"

Mam gazed at him thoughtfully then nodded. "I'll heat up the water for tea."

Katie parked her family's buggy on Evan Bontrager's property and sat quietly, needing a moment before she could get out and face Jacob's family. She was nervous and felt awful that she hadn't spent any time with her betrothed's family in the months since Jacob's funeral. They'd seen each other at church functions, but other than a wave or a quick hello, she'd kept her distance. Seeing them at first had brought back the pain of her loss. *I loved his family. I should have stopped by for a visit.*

She glanced at the cherry pie on the bench seat behind her. Katie thought that Micah would appreciate another baked item besides a pound cake. If he didn't like it, other members within the family would eat it.

A knock on the back then the side of the buggy startled her. She turned as a man popped up in her open side window. Matt Bontrager. She couldn't help returning his grin.

"Katie!" He popped the door and reached in to grab her. She could see the difference one year had made in the teenager. Matt seemed to be more handsome at eighteen than he was at seventeen. He'd always been a charmer, but now his muscled arms, sparkling eyes and wide smile would soon be breaking hearts all over the county.

He easily picked her up and set her on her feet next to the buggy. "It's *gut* to see you, *schweschter*." His dark eyes so different than Jacob's or Micah's studied her intently. "You've lost weight." He took stock of her from head to toe. "We've missed you, Katie."

Katie opened her mouth, closed it. She cracked a smile. "I missed you—all of you," she admitted. And she had. More than she'd realized.

"Katie?" Vernon, the youngest Bontrager brother, approached more shyly. He wasn't as welcoming as Matt.

"Vern," she murmured. "You've grown at least six inches in the last year."

One side of his mouth tipped upward. "Time has a way of changing us," he said, his gaze warming.

She studied Vernon, noting that the sixteen-year-old looked more like a full-grown man than the boy she'd first met. Like his brothers, he was handsome.

Her gaze went to the house, and Katie experienced a nervous flutter in her belly.

"Go on in, Katie," Vern said. "Micah is waiting for you with my nephew and nieces."

Katie nodded then reached in for the pie on the front passenger side. She straightened while holding the plate carefully.

"You baked for us, Katie?" Matt asked.

"*Nay*, she baked for Micah," Vern grumbled. "Just like the pound cake he'd barely allowed us a taste of."

Katie gazed at the pie then looked up to zero her gaze in on Vern. "He liked the pound cake?"

"I'll say." Matt made a face. "We each got a thin slice, but he and his *kinner* ate the rest of it." He smiled. "It was delicious!"

Unable to help herself, Katie chuckled.

"What kind of pie did you make?" Vern asked.

"Cherry." With pie in hand, she stepped away from the buggy to close the door.

"We'll not get any of that," Matt complained. "It's Micah's favorite."

Warmth filled Katie's chest. "I'm glad I made something to be enjoyed."

"Why don't you give us each a taste now?" Matt reached for the dessert but Katie kept it away from him.

The slam of the screened door had Katie's gaze shooting toward the house. She smiled as twenty-year-old Jonathan, a year younger than Jacob had been when he'd courted her, approached, his eyebrows raising as he saw his brothers standing on either side of Katie.

Unlike Vern and Matt who had dark hair but

brown eyes, Jonathan had blond hair and eyes the same color as Jacob, whose eyes were a paler blue than Micah's. As Jonathan approached, Katie closed her eyes and breathed in to calm herself while shutting out thoughts of her deceased fiancé.

"Katie," Jonathan greeted, not as open as the other brothers.

"*Hallo*, Jonathan. I hear you're working with Peter Troyer. How is that going?"

The man's expression softened. "It's going well. I enjoy working with him."

"I'm glad." She sensed someone on the back stoop and glanced over. As if waiting for her, Micah stood with a baby in his arms. "I…it's *wunderbor* to see you," she said to the three brothers. "I'm glad to know that you are all doing well."

She heard them telling her that they would see her later as she started toward the house where Micah waited. She suddenly felt shaky inside and prayed that she wouldn't trip and make a fool of herself. As she drew near, she saw that there was no smile of welcome. Her heart started to beat rapidly, and her hands holding the pie felt damp and clammy.

Katie continued right up to the back stoop where she halted and looked up at him. "*Hallo*, Micah." Today he was dressed in a spring-green shirt and navy pants with matching suspenders. He wore no hat since he'd come from inside the house.

Micah nodded, then stepped aside and opened the door for her, allowing her to precede him inside. She immediately detected the clean scent of soap and another fragrance that must belong only to him. His light brown hair was nicely combed and covered just the tips of his ears. His beard was clean, neatly groomed and not as long as the older married men with their gray beards. He had an attractive face with a nose that was like Jacob's but not. His brown lashes were long for a man, framing eyes of a blue that was startling in its intensity.

She waited for him to close the door behind him before she handed him the pie. "I hope you like cherry pie."

Micah stared at the pie before his gaze settled on her face. She couldn't tell what he was thinking as the two locked gazes. "How did you know that cherry is my favorite?"

Katie relaxed and smiled when she saw the sudden stunned, pleased look on his face. "I didn't know. I like cherry pie so I hoped you did, too."

"I do. *Danki*." A small smile curved Micah's lips and she felt the impact of his softening expression. He shifted the little girl in his arms.

"Who do we have here?" Katie asked, beaming at the sweet face of a child who looked no older than a year, if she was even that.

Micah gazed at his daughter with a smile. "This is Eliza."

The bubbel. She moved closer to catch the child's eye. When beautiful blue eyes encountered hers, Katie smiled and held out her arms. To her delight, Eliza leaned forward as if eager to be held by her. Katie immediately cuddled the baby girl. The child smelled clean and sweet, and Katie was happy to have the privilege of holding her. Eliza made a coo of delight when

Katie turned her to face her, and the child grinned at her. "You're a delight, Eliza Bontrager."

Conscious of Micah's gaze, Katie glanced up at him with a smile on her lips that quickly died when she saw his expression. Was he unhappy that Eliza was quick to accept her?

Katie ran her hand down the child's back. "How old is she again?"

"One." Micah placed a hand on his son's shoulder. "Jacob is three."

She stilled as she studied the little boy. He didn't look at all like her Jacob, and she relaxed with a smile for him. "*Hallo*, Jacob. I'm Katie."

The boy's father frowned when Jacob didn't immediately say anything. "Jacob? Say *hallo* to Katie. She's a friend of the family."

Jacob looked up at his father before he left Micah's side to stand in front of Katie. "*Gut* morning, Katie," he said politely.

Katie smiled, and to her amazement, the boy smiled back at her. She returned her attention to Micah. "You have three *kinner*. Where is your other *dochter*?"

"Kat-ie," a little voice said, and Katie turned, only just then noticing the little girl seated in a high chair in the far corner.

She approached the child. "You must be Rebecca," she said softly, studying the girl with warmth. "Are you eating a muffin?" The young one nodded. It wasn't hard to see that she was since there were muffin crumbs and pieces all over the tray in front of her. "Hmmm, what kind?" Katie leaned closer. "Chocolate chip?"

Rebecca hit the high chair tray with her two hands, scattering and smearing crumbs onto the flat surface. *"Chip, chip, chip."*

Katie felt Micah close behind her. She turned and watched as he went to the kitchen drawer, pulled out a washcloth, then used it to wipe Rebecca's face and hands. He pulled the tray out enough to lift his daughter from the high chair. Katie saw the mess on the tray, grabbed the cloth and cleaned it up before she used a tea towel to dry it.

The kettle on the stove whistled. Movement in the doorway to the great room drew Katie's attention to Betty, who stood uncertainly at the edge of the kitchen before she moved to the stove and turned off the flame. Katie smiled and, still with Eliza in her arms, moved to greet her properly.

"Betty," she breathed, fighting tears. She had always loved Jacob's mother and now she felt bad for not spending time with her sooner.

Betty blinked and her eyes glistened with emotion. "Katie."

Katie drew the woman close with her free hand. "It's been too long," she said softly. "I'm sorry."

"I've missed you," Betty said.

"I've missed you, too. I saw Matt, Vern and Jonathan outside. I've seen them all from a distance, but they have matured into fine young men."

A snort of derision drew her attention to Micah, who eyed her with good humor. "You obviously haven't seen them misbehave at the table. Or act like children when they fight over a dessert."

Katie stared at him. "Like pound cake?"

To her surprise, she saw his cheeks turn bright red. "That and other things. And no matter what they told you, I did share the cake with them. We each had an equal-sized piece."

The laughter that came unbidden from her mouth startled her as much as it did Micah and Betty. "I'll make two next time." She smiled at Micah. "You can keep one for yourself over at the *haus*."

Micah's smile hit her like a ton of bricks. "Would you like some hot tea?"

Katie nodded. "I'd love one." Betty pulled cups out of the cabinet. "Why don't you sit down and I'll take care of it."

"You were always a sweet girl," Betty said.

She chuckled. "I'm not sure my brothers and sisters will agree with you."

Micah put Rebecca back in her chair then reached for Eliza and placed her in a second high chair that was behind the table, leaving Katie free to fix their tea. She turned and watched as he then lifted Jacob onto a kitchen chair and pushed it under the table before handing him sheets of paper and crayons so that his son could draw pictures.

Micah locked gazes with Katie as she turned with the tea she'd made. She blushed then looked away and set the cups carefully on the table.

"Do you still take sugar without milk in your tea?" she asked Mam.

"Ja." His mother smiled. "You remembered."

She is a lovely woman, and someone who most likely knows my family better than I do. He'd stayed behind after his family had left Michigan for Pennsylvania two years ago. He'd known he couldn't ask Anna to leave her family and friends because of his parents' choice to move. So he, Anna and their little ones had stayed in Centreville. Since their departure, his parents had visited him and Anna once right after Rebecca was born.

"How are your *mudder* and *vadder*?" Mam asked Katie.

"They are *gut*. They keep busy. My siblings are a handful for Mam." Katie took a drink from her tea then gave her attention to Micah. "Would you like a piece of your cherry pie?"

"You made him a cherry pie?" Mam said with a smile.

"She did." He narrowed his gaze on his mother. "You didn't tell her it's my favorite, did you?" He saw Katie stiffen. She'd already told him that she didn't know cherry pies were his favorite when she'd given it to him. "I believe you didn't know, but that doesn't mean Mam didn't put a bug in your *mudder*'s ear."

Her expression tight, she looked at him. "My *mam* wasn't home when I made the pie earlier."

"I apologize. I didn't mean…" Micah felt flustered in a woman's presence for the first time. He hadn't experienced such strange feelings when he'd first met his late wife.

Katie tilted her head as she studied him. They locked gazes, and she must have read regret in his expression as she suddenly smiled. "I'm glad you like it," she said. "Do you want a piece? Or would you rather wait until after lunch?"

He shifted his eyes to his mother, who was watching with a small smile of amusement on her lips.

"You're a grown man and a father. If you want some, eat it," Mam said.

Turning back to Katie, he nodded. "I would love a piece of pie."

She rose, found two plates in a wall cabinet easily, which showed him how at home she had been when Jacob had been alive. "Betty, would you like a piece?"

Betty was silent for a moment. "Why not? Let's taste your cherry pie. If it's anything like your other baked goods, it will be delicious."

Micah watched Katie cut two slices before giving one to him and one to his mother. "Aren't you having a piece?" he asked.

"*Nay*. It's your pie."

"Actually, it's yours. You made it." Micah said with a twinkle in his blue eyes. "Have a slice if you want it."

"*Nay. Danki*. I'm not certain it's safe to eat," she said as he took a big bite and began to chew. He froze instantly and stared at her with horror. She laughed out loud, and he was enchanted with the joy and good humor on her beautiful features.

Mam gazed at Katie, looking pleased. "It's *gut* to hear your laughter, *dochter*."

"I'm sorry," she began, becoming subdued.

"*Nay*, I love seeing you enjoy life again," Mam said. "'Tis been too long."

As he went back to eating his pie, which tasted delicious, he knew he'd have to hide it from his brothers if he was to enjoy a second piece. She felt his gaze on her and looked up. Katie's eyes crinkled as she grinned at him.

"So now that you've met these little ones," Betty said, "are you still willing to watch them for Micah?"

"*Ja*, I would be happy to watch them." Katie smiled as she looked at his daughters in their high chairs, each sharing a small serving of pie from their grandmother's plate. Then she focused her attention on his son. "Jacob, would you like a little cherry pie?"

Jacob, who had been bent over his drawing with his tongue between his lips, lifted his head and looked up at her. "Can I have another muffin instead?"

"What kind would you like?" Mam rose to grab the muffins that had been wrapped up and left on the kitchen counter.

"Cimmamim?"

"Cinnamon," Micah corrected.

His son nodded. "*Ja*, cimmamim," he said with a grin.

Micah laughed. He couldn't help himself. He caught Katie's glance and saw her warm expression and the approval in her blue eyes. And he experienced a sensation of warmth inside his chest as he held her gaze.

He understood what had drawn Jacob's attention. There was something riveting about Katie Mast. She'd told him that she would never marry again, which was a shame. He could envision her as a wife and mother of many children. She was different from Anna. Like Katie, he didn't want to marry again, but unlike her, he had no choice. Although this was only the second time he'd spent any time with her, he got the feeling that he could trust her. *With his children.*

And maybe—just maybe—they could be friends.

Chapter Four

Katie woke up, gasping, heart racing. She'd dreamt of the accident again with Jacob lying in the farm field prone and bloody. Katie never saw Jacob after the accident. No one would let her see him, so since learning what had happened to her beloved betrothed, her mind had filled with horrific images of how Jacob must have suffered, how awful the accident must have been.

Throwing off the top sheet, she got out of bed then quickly made it. Still shaky after the nightmare, she dressed, pinned her hair and put on her head covering. "Jacob," she murmured, blinking back tears. "I miss you."

Was she dreaming of Jacob again because she'd met Micah, his older brother? Someone who looked so much like the man she'd loved and lost that she'd nearly fainted when she'd first set eyes on him? A father with three children. A widower. *A Bontrager.*

She paused a moment to close her eyes and breathe deeply. Jacob was gone. She had no other choice but to go on. Katie waited until she felt composed again and then headed downstairs to help her mother with breakfast for her father and five siblings. Her younger sisters Abigail, seventeen, and Ruthann, fifteen, were already in the kitchen when Katie entered the room. They had set the long trestle table large enough for her family. Her mother stood near the stove, cooking eggs and bacon.

"*Gut* morning!" Ruthann greeted, seeing Katie first.

"*Gut* morning, Ruthann. Everyone," Katie said. "I'm sorry I'm late."

"Didn't you sleep well?" Mam asked as she flipped the bacon in the cast-iron frying pan.

"I slept." Katie went to the refrigerator to pull out butter and jam then placed them on the table. As she started to slice a loaf of bread, she could feel her mother's gaze. She tried to smile at her.

"You *oll recht*?" Mam stirred the eggs then turned off the heat.

"I'm fine." Katie placed the slices of bread into a cloth-covered basket and set them on the table near the butter and jam. "Where are our *bruders*?"

"Outside taking care of the animals," Ruthann said. "At least Abe is."

Katie could control a grin despite still feeling the aftereffects of her bad dream. Her youngest brother, Abraham, was responsible and kind at twelve years old. "What about Joseph and Uri?"

"Joseph is with Dat," Abigail told her. "Uri hasn't come downstairs yet, but I know he's awake as I heard him in his room earlier."

She eyed her sister thoughtfully as she considered her eighteen-year-old brother. Uri was the oldest son and three years younger than her. Was he well? She'd sensed that something had been bothering him lately. *But what?* She, as the most senior of her parents' children, should try to have a talk with him later, when the opportunity presented itself.

Mam dumped the eggs onto a plate and placed the crispy strips of bacon onto a platter. She covered the plates to keep them warm and started to cook more of both. "Katie, would you pour coffee for your father and Uri?" she asked as she finished up the eggs and bacon.

"*Ja*, Mam." Katie took four mugs out of the cabinet, one each for her father, her brothers Uri and Joseph and herself. "Would you like tea?" she asked her mother.

"I think I'll just have juice," Mam said as she set the food in the center of the table. As if the scent of breakfast drew everyone from outside, Dat, Joseph and Abraham entered through the back door.

"Smells *gut* in here," Dat said, eyeing the food.

Uri entered from the great room and quietly took a seat.

"*Gut* morning, Uri," Katie said softly as she made up a plate and set it in front of him.

Uri met her gaze. *"Danki,"* he murmured.

"You didn't come out to help with the animals," Abe accused with a look at his eldest brother.

"Abraham," Mam said quietly. "I need Uri's help with a plumbing problem upstairs."

Katie hid a smile as she saw the quick, surprised look on Uri's face.

"I could have done it for you, Sarah," her father chimed in.

"Merv," her mother said softly, "you have enough to keep you busy."

Dat nodded. *"Soohn,"* he addressed Uri, "if you want help, just let me know. *Ja?"*

Uri nodded.

There was a knock on the back door, and everyone turned as Abe opened it to reveal Betty and Evan Bontrager. The first thing that captured Katie's attention as the couple entered the house was Micah's resemblance to his father with his brown hair and bright blue eyes. Jacob's coloring had been similar, but his blue eyes were a lighter shade than Evan and Micah's bright blue.

"Hallo!" Mam said with a smile as she got up from the table. "Breakfast? Joseph, can you pull a few chairs in from the other room?" She had made enough to feed more than her family.

"No need. We already ate." Evan grinned with warmth. "Betty made biscuits and gravy."

"Ja, we can't stay long," Betty said. "We wanted to invite you for Visiting Day this Sunday. You'll come, *ja?"* Her gaze fell on Katie briefly then slipped over to Mam. "Sarah?"

"We will be there," Dat said before Mam could answer.

Katie's heart stuttered in her chest. She wouldn't mind going. The thought of seeing Micah again made her nervous, but if she was going to watch his children while he worked then she needed to learn to interact with him.

"Coffee? Tea?" she asked Jacob's parents.

"*Danki*, but *nay*. We have a few errands to run," Betty said. Her blond hair and hazel eyes made an unusual combination in the Bontrager family. Her spring dress was a shade lighter than her husband's short-sleeved shirt.

"Micah working on the *haus* today?" Katie asked casually, the mention of his name causing a flutter in her stomach.

"*Ja*, he is. Emma and Addie are with the children, so I don't want to be gone long," Betty said.

"The children seemed content with your *dechter*," Katie said.

"They are *gut* with them," Betty agreed with a nod. She exchanged glances with her husband, before turning back to address Katie's family. "We'll see you on Sunday then."

"What would you like me to bring?" Mam said.

"I can bake some desserts," Katie offered.

Betty smiled. "That sounds wonderful."

Mam glanced at Katie before turning back to Betty. "*I'll* make potato salad and coleslaw, if that's *oll recht*," she said.

Jacob and Micah's mother grinned. "We'll look forward to it."

Dat followed them outside and talked for a bit with Evan before he returned to his seat to finish breakfast. "It will be *gut* to spend time with them again."

Katie immediately felt guilty for keeping the families apart. "I'm sorry," she said, meeting her father's then her mother's gazes.

"You have nothing to feel sorry about, *dochter*," Dat said.

"It's my fault that you haven't spent enough time with them."

"Katie," Mam said, "I've had tea with Betty a couple of times this past month. We know you've been grieving and have every right to be. Knowing that you're willing to take care of Micah's children makes things easier for us all to get together." Her gaze softened as she studied Katie. "We hated to see you hurting, but I truly understand why you couldn't see Jacob's family."

"Mam…"

"We'll not be pressing you, *dochter*."

Katie released a powerful breath. "Anyone want more coffee or juice?"

Uri held his mug to her. She smiled at him and filled it. "Dat?" she asked.

Her father shook his head. "Had enough this morning. This wasn't my first cup." His blue eyes focused on her until her brother Abraham drew his attention.

"Are we going into town today?" Abe asked.

"*Ja,*" Dat said. "We need feed." His gaze found another brother. "Joseph, you going to come with us?"

"*Ja*, why not?"

"Uri?"

He stared at his plate before meeting his father's eyes. "I've got plumbing to fix for Mam."

As her family made plans around the table, Katie thought of what she needed to do today. She had sewing items to deliver to Kings General Store. Over the last two days, she'd made cooking aprons, a baby quilt and a number of prayer *kapps*. Visiting Day was in three days. As she sipped the last of her coffee, she thought about what type of desserts she would make Saturday morning for Sunday to enjoy after the midday meal. *Cherry pie and pound cake.* She recalled how much the Bontrager family, especially Micah, had enjoyed both treats. She wanted to make a third dessert but wasn't sure what to take yet. A coffee cake? Shoo-fly pie? She had a little time to think about it. Whatever she made, she hoped that everyone would enjoy it.

Saturday morning dawned clear and bright. Katie stepped outside to think for a few moments before she returned to the kitchen to check on the cake and pie she'd put in the oven, the desserts she'd promised to take to the Evan Bontragers the next day.

She drew in a breath as she stood in the barnyard, enjoying a quick fresh inhale of late summer air. The squeak of the door behind her drew her attention as Uri stepped outside. "Uri."

He nodded. "Katie."

She studied him intently, noting the lackluster look in his brown eyes. "What's going on with you, *bruder*?" It was the first opportunity she had to speak with her brother alone. "You can talk to me. I won't tell anyone. I'm your *schweschter*, and I can tell when something is wrong."

Uri met her gaze with a sigh. "You won't tell anyone?"

"You have my word," Katie told him.

"Emma."

"Emma Bontrager? Micah's little sister? She is about fifteen, *ja*?"

He nodded. "Almost sixteen. She'll be sixteen next month."

Katie watched the myriad of expressions cross her brother's face. "You like her."

He ran a hand across his nape. He wore no hat, and his dark hair looked as if he'd run his fingers through it multiple times in the last hour. "*Ja*, I like her."

"What is the problem then?"

"She doesn't like me."

She frowned. "How do you know that?"

"By the way she's acting." He scowled. "And now we're going over to the Bontragers on Sunday. I know she'll ignore me. She's acted odd at church singings every time I approached so I just walked away. And whenever our paths cross, she refuses to look at me. The other day I went to the store for Mam and I saw her. She pretended she didn't see me, but I know she did. Our gazes found each other before she turned away."

She laughed. "She likes you, Uri. If she didn't, she'd meet your gaze and say *hallo* then move on. She wouldn't do her best to avoid you. I have a feeling that she is nervous around you because she likes you, too."

Uri's brown eyes brightened. "You think so?"

"I do."

He grinned before the good humor left his expression. "So what should I do?"

"You can ignore her and see what she does. Maybe she'll hate that. Maybe she'll seek you out to talk with you."

"*Danki*, Katie."

"I don't know if she'll do that, Uri, even if she does like you." She eyed her brother affectionately. "You're *willkomm*, *bruder*." She faced him fully. "Let me know how it turns out, *ja*?"

"*Oll recht*."

An hour later, Katie took the golden-brown pound cake from the oven and set it on top of the stove. She then reached in for the cherry pie. The crumb topping covering the fruit looked perfect. The rich smell of cooked cherries filled the air as she set the pie carefully on a hot mat on the kitchen counter. She made a fresh peach cobbler as well, as she wasn't sure how many families would be at the Bontragers visiting. The cobbler wouldn't be as good tomorrow as eating it fresh from the oven, but she figured it would be delicious anyway since she'd bought peaches from a local orchard.

It was quiet in the house. Her sisters had gone out for the day. Two of her brothers were in the barn cleaning the stables. Her father was visiting a friend on the other side of New Berne. Her mother was at the store with her youngest brother, Abraham. Mam had decided to make more salads for Visiting Day than what she'd told Betty.

Katie finished the desserts and put them on a shelf in the mud room to cool. She'd have to watch to ensure her siblings didn't get into the sweets before tomorrow. Anticipating the visit made her think of

Micah and his children. She looked forward to babysitting Jacob, Rebecca and Eliza. She loved young ones and now that she wasn't going to have any of her own…

She thought of her betrothed. Jacob had treated her well, wonderfully in fact. His smile frequently had lit up his expression, especially when he'd set eyes on her. Katie felt a pang in the region of her heart. *Why did you work in the fields alone that day, Jacob?*

"I guess I'll never know why," she murmured as she removed her apron and put it in the laundry. She cleaned up the kitchen then went up to her room. Suddenly, the house felt too quiet. The silence left her with thoughts she longed to forget but knew she never would. Not when it came to Jacob Bontrager. The man she'd loved and wanted a future with. *Why, Jacob? Why?*

Sunday morning Dat drove the family to the Bontrager residence. Katie held the cake and pie on her lap while her sister Abigail held on to the cobbler. The Bontragers lived less than fifteen minutes away. Katie felt butterflies in her stomach as her father drove past farms close to the Bontragers' property. When Dat pulled into the lot, the butterflies became more active, almost painful, as she grew increasingly nervous. It wasn't the family that made feel her way. It was the thought of seeing Micah again. She was convinced that seeing Micah look like a much older version of Jacob had triggered the accident nightmare.

The screen door on the side entrance flew open, and Vernon and Matthew burst out of the house. *"Hallo!"* Matthew called with a grin.

Katie waited for her parents to get out of the buggy first before she got out carefully, holding the two desserts. "Matthew, how are you?"

"Fine, fine!" His dark eyes gleamed as he studied her. "It's *gut* to see you again, Katie."

"Hallo, Katie. Ruthann." Vernon said, blushing when her sister said *hallo*. Ruthann was just a year younger than him. He transferred his attention to Katie and reached to take the cake and pie from her. "I'll take these into the house."

"Danki, Vern," she said with a smile.

Jonathan came out to join his brothers. He approached Abigail with a small smile. *"Hallo,* Abigail. May I take that from you?" he asked, referring to the peach cobbler.

"I don't know," she teased. "Are you going to eat it or wait until after the midday meal when everyone gets to have a taste?"

"You can trust me," he said, blue eyes twinkling, pale unlike Micah's and his father's.

Abigail nodded and handed it over. Jonathan grinned at her and raced toward the house. "I've got peach cobbler!" he shouted with a look over his shoulder at her. Abbie laughed and walked toward the house with Ruthann and Abraham.

Katie waited until Uri approached more slowly. She placed a hand on his arm without a word, and Uri smiled slightly as they walked together toward the house.

They hadn't gotten far when the door opened again, and Micah stood in the opening with his baby daughter Eliza on his hip. Katie halted briefly as her heartbeat spiked, drawing Uri's attention. When she saw the welcome on Micah's handsome features, she pulled herself together, nodded at Uri, and then brother and sister continued the rest of the way to the house. Micah stepped back to allow them entry.

"*Hallo*, Micah," Katie said pleasantly as she brushed by him.

"Katie. We're glad that you could visit today."

"I'm glad, too." She swallowed against a suddenly tight throat. "I've missed your family." Looking away from him, she experienced a moment of sadness and guilt. "I shouldn't have stayed away so long." She could feel Micah's gaze on her.

"I understand," he said sincerely, and Katie shot him a glance as she realized that he most likely did. He tragically had lost his wife. Had he avoided his wife's family because it'd been too painful after she'd passed away?

"Katie!" Emma Bontrager looked happy to see her.

"Emma, it's *gut* to see you!" Just then Uri entered the house, and Katie saw a change in Emma's demeanor.

"*Gut* morning, Emma," Uri said softly.

"Uri," she said stiffly.

Katie looked at each one's expression and wondered what she could do, if anything, to ease the tension between them. She glanced toward Micah to see if he noticed the exchange between Uri and his sister

Emma, but Micah's attention had been drawn away by his father. Katie saw him walk into the other room with his daughter, and she relaxed.

Soon, she and Uri were surrounded by their own family members as well as numerous Bontrager siblings. Emma was pleased to see Ruthann. The two girls were the same age.

Katie blew out a breath. By the end of the day, things would be fine, she told herself. She would get used to being around Micah and his family. She saw Micah's son Jacob run up to his uncle Matthew. Matt hefted him high into the air, and the little boy's giggles made Katie's heart light up. She loved children. She might not have any of her own, but her siblings would no doubt marry, and she would be a good aunt to them. But until then she'd have to be content to enjoy Micah's children once they moved into the renovated house and she spent her days watching them while Micah worked.

Chapter Five

Katie stood at the kitchen window, peering out into the backyard as she unwrapped two large bowls of cold salads for the midday meal. She'd been glad to learn that her family were the only ones visiting. Despite her initial nervousness, she enjoyed catching up with the Bontragers who had come to mean so much to her after Jacob had brought her home to get to know them. She smiled. Today she even felt a new easiness around Micah.

Her brothers and the Bontrager brothers, except for Micah, were playing baseball on the back lawn. The women and girls were in the kitchen getting the food ready. Micah watched from his chair with Eliza and Rebecca on his lap, far enough away from the game to be safe from fly balls. Young Jacob sat on a patchwork quilt next to his father. It was a sunny summer's day with clear blue skies—wonderful weather for enjoying a lovely outing. Katie's father and Evan Bontrager had worked together to construct eating tables from wooden sawhorses and plywood.

A long white plastic folding table had been set up in the backyard for the food.

Katie reached in a kitchen drawer for serving utensils and pulled out two large spoons. She put a spoon in each bowl and glanced outside again, grinning as she listened to her brothers' enthusiasm for playing ball.

"Micah!" her brother Abraham shouted. "Why don't you come play with us?"

"*Danki*, but I can't right now," Micah said, and she saw the tiny smile he gave to his children.

"Boys," Betty called through the screen door leading to the kitchen. "You can go back to your ball game after we eat."

"Food!" Matthew Bontrager shouted, appearing eager as he tossed the baseball up in the air and caught it as he headed toward the food table. "I'm hungry!"

"You're always hungry," his brother Jonathan teased with a laugh.

"You're all always hungry," his sister Emma said, sticking her head out the door to see where their fathers had set the tables, which Betty and Sarah, Katie's mother, had covered with sheets as tablecloths.

Everyone laughed at Emma's comment, even Micah. Katie settled her gaze on him with his children and felt a little tug on her heartstrings. If things had been different, the man would have been her brother-in-law and his children her nephew and nieces. She quickly blinked back tears and turned away from the window. "I'm going to take these outside," she said of the two salads in her arms. "I'll be back to help carry out the rest."

"Wait up," Emma said, "and I'll walk out with you." The fifteen-year-old held a platter of cold roast beef.

Katie smiled as the girl joined her, and they went outside together. "It's *gut* to spend time with you, Emma," she said as they headed toward the food table. "I can't believe how much you've changed since…"

"I know," Emma said softly. "Things—people—change."

"I'm sorry I didn't come by sooner. It was just too—"

"Painful," the girl said. "I understand. But, Katie, we missed you. Our *bruder* loved you and we do, too. After you were gone, we felt as if we also lost you."

Fighting tears, Katie nodded. "I'm sorry," she whispered. "I promise to be better about visiting. *Oll recht?*"

Emma grinned. "I would like that."

Katie set the bowls of macaroni salad and potato salad at one end of the food table and watched Emma place the platter of meat in the center. Ruthann left the house carrying a platter of cold ham. Emma stayed to chat with Katie's sister as Katie headed back to the house. She was conscious of Micah's eyes on her as she passed him to climb the porch steps. Emma headed inside with Ruthann after allowing Betty to pass with a plate of cheese and crackers.

"I'll take that," Katie offered, reaching for snacks.

"*Danki*, Katie." Betty smiled as she gave Katie the plate then headed into the house.

After setting it down outside, Katie turned to

find Micah watching her intently. On impulse, she stopped before him. "If you'd like to play baseball with our *bruders* later, I'll be happy to watch your little ones," she said.

The little uptick of his lips made her heart beat faster. "That's kind of you."

"It will be *gut* experience," she managed. "With you being here while I... Ah, then you'll see you can trust me with them."

"I already do." His blue eyes watched her carefully as if trying to gauge her reaction. A tiny smile blossomed on his face. "I accept your offer," he said, "and not because I need to see the way you handle my *kinner*. I could tell immediately the first time I saw you with them that you are *gut* with *kinner*." He stood with his two youngest cradled within his arms. She saw the flex of his forearm muscles as he shifted to allow Eliza, his sleepy baby, to become more comfortable.

Katie felt her lips curve. *"Danki,"* she said softly. Her gaze fell softly on Eliza. "Do you want me to put her down for a nap?"

"I think I should get her to eat first."

She nodded in understanding. The way Micah continued to study her made her wonder if she had a few stray hairs. She started to reach up to her *kapp* to check when he grinned.

"You look perfect," he whispered. "Not a hair out of place."

She could feel her cheeks heat as she glanced away. "I should go inside and help bring out the rest of food so we can eat." She took a few steps toward the house.

"Katie?"

She spun, stunned to hear him calling her. *"Ja?"*

"Danki for your offer," he said. "To watch my *kinner."*

Flustered by the intensity of his gaze, Katie needed a minute to answer. When his gaze softened, she relaxed. "You're *willkomm*," she murmured then hurried into the house.

Within minutes, the women had the food set up on the table outside. Her *dat*, Evan and their sons got up first to fill their plates.

"Mervin, I can fill a plate for you," *Mam* said, drawing Katie's attention.

"Nay, Sarah," *Dat* replied with a smile for his wife. "Get yourself a plate and enjoy your meal. You don't need to wait on me."

Listening to her parents' exchange, Katie experienced a warmth. She knew they loved each other but hearing the affection in their voices touched her deeply. Not every couple who married had the kind of relationship they did. *I would have enjoyed it with Jacob.* Sighing, she grabbed a plate and got at the end of the food line.

"You made cherry pie and pound cake," a familiar masculine voice murmured suddenly from behind her.

Spine tingling, Katie turned and met Micah's gaze. "Your family seemed to enjoy them so I thought they would be a *gut* choice to bring," she told him. "I enjoy baking and can make other things as well."

"What's next to the pound cake on the left?" he asked, gesturing toward a square baking dish at the other end of the table.

"Peach cobbler," she told him, following his gaze toward dish in question. "It tastes better warm, but the peaches are fresh."

"Miller's Orchard?" he asked.

She nodded.

"Their peaches are delicious," he said. "I think I'll have a taste of your cobbler." He shifted behind her, making her overly aware of him.

He stood alone, and she wondered where his children were. Then she saw that Emma had Rebecca on her lap while Addie held Eliza. Her sister Abigail was giving young Jacob tidbits of food from her plate.

"Have you gotten a lot done on the *haus*?" she asked, meeting his gaze again.

"Well…" he replied, sounding pleased. "I finished the kitchen and laundry areas, and now I've switched to renovations to the upstairs bedrooms and bathroom."

"What do you have to do?" she asked as she moved down the line, adding a small spoonful of each salad to her plate.

"I need to paint and replace the floors," he said, taking salad as Katie added a helping of chowchow, a pickled mixture of garden vegetables, to her plate.

"Wood floors or vinyl?"

"Vinyl," he said. "At least in Jacob's and the girls' rooms. Easier to maintain when dealing with children's messes. I haven't decided about the main bedroom yet."

Katie nodded. Sheet vinyl was a common choice for floors in Amish houses because they were easy to keep clean. She wondered what pattern he'd chosen or if he'd yet to choose one. She forked a piece of roast beef onto her plate then handed the serving fork to Micah.

"Danki," he murmured. He added two slices of roast beef to his plate and continued along the line behind Katie.

Katie eyed the ham and decided that she had enough on her plate. She turned to head back to her table when she accidentally brushed against Micah's arm as he moved down the line. "Sorry," she mumbled, moving out of his way.

He grinned at her. "Enjoy your lunch, Katie." Then he continued down the table to finish loading his plate with food.

Katie sat with her sisters, her brothers and Addie Bontrager, who came over to eat with them. There were two tables, set up short end to short end, creating a large family eating area. Matthew and Vernon had joined them at their end, and they chatted about events happening in their lives. While she ate slowly, listening to the others talk, she was conscious of Micah's gaze. She looked over but he'd turned his attention to his mother beside him. Mam and Dat sat close to Betty and Evan with Jonathan next to his father and his sisters Emma and Sarie seated across the table from them.

"I'm going to get some dessert before it's all gone," Katie said as she stood. "Anyone want anything?"

"Will you see if there is any pound cake left?" Matt asked.

"*Ja*, I'll be happy to."

His sister Addie rose to her feet. "I'll go with you." She glanced toward Katie's brother Uri. "Would you like a piece of cake or pie?" she asked him casually, but Katie recognized something in her expression that made her think that Addie was sweet on Uri.

Uri met the girl's gaze and shook his head. "*Nay*, I had plenty."

Katie sighed. If only her brother liked Addie instead of Emma, he would be much happier.

Soon the meal was over, and Katie helped the women clean up. When she was finished, she hurried outside to see if Micah wanted her to watch the children while he played ball. As she approached, she heard Micah and his sister Emma talking.

"I'll put them down for their naps," Emma said, and Katie saw that the children looked sleepy.

Micah saw Katie's approach. "Let Katie help you with them," he said.

Emma spun, saw Katie and smiled. "*Ja*. Katie? Would you mind helping me to get these little ones upstairs to bed?"

"My pleasure." She met Micah's gaze to see him watching her thoughtfully.

Emma reached for Rebecca, and Micah carefully slipped little Eliza into Katie's arms. "We'll come back for Jacob, *bruder*," Emma said.

"Jacob, go with Katie upstairs," Micah told his son, surprising her.

"*Dat*, I'm not tired."

Micah studied him. "*Ja*, you are. Lie down like a *gut boo*, and I'll make sure you get a special treat when you wake up."

"Some more pound cake?"

"If there is any left."

"Jacob," Katie said softly. "I'll make you another one if you take a nap for me."

"You will?" He narrowed his eyes as he gazed up at her.

"*Ja*, I made this one—and the one you had the other day."

He blinked, smiled then held out his hand to her. *"Oke."*

With the baby cradled in one arm, Katie took Jacob by the hand and, with a last quick look at the boy's father, led him toward the house behind Emma. The boy's fingers was small and warm clasped within her own. She felt a wave of affection for the child, her Jacob's namesake. Katie thought of the children she would have had with her deceased betrothed and experienced a moment of sadness, which she dispelled as they continued toward the stairs.

Emma led her to a second-story bedroom where there was a crib and a toddler bed. Emma laid Rebecca down carefully and smiled when the little girl continued to sleep.

Katie released Jacob's hand and was impressed when he waited quietly for her to place baby Eliza in her crib. She loved how Eliza curled up on her side and kept snoozing. When she turned, she found Jacob watching her thoughtfully. "Now it's your turn," she said.

Emma grinned at her as they left the room. "Want me to help?" she asked.

Shaking her head, Katie glanced at Jacob. *"Nay,*

it's fine. I'll be down soon." She turned to Jacob. "Will you show me where you sleep?"

Jacob nodded, released Katie's hand and led the way to another room where there was a large bed and a smaller one. "I sleep here with *Dat*," he told her.

"It's a nice room," she said, feeling strange as she eyed its contents. A blue shirt and black felt wide-brimmed hat hung on wall hooks next to a dresser on the other side of the room.

"Did you really make the pound cake we had today?" he asked, watching her.

"I did. I made the cherry pie and peach cobbler, too."

"I like pound cake." He continued to study her with innocent blue eyes.

"Me, too. I'll make you one tomorrow then ensure you get some, *ja*?"

He bobbed his head. Jacob then climbed onto his bed.

"Do you want the shade drawn?" Katie asked. "The sun is bright."

Jacob shook his head. "Can we leave it up?"

"Ja." She took off his shoes, watched as he settled in, then straightened. "Sleep well, Jacob."

"Danki, Katie, for the pound cake."

"You're *willkomm*, little one." Katie slipped out of the room and went downstairs.

The children were still sleeping when Katie and her family said their goodbyes. Micah pulled her aside as she started toward the buggy.

"I'll let you know when we move into the *haus*,"

he told her, his deep voice having a strange effect on her.

She nodded. "*Oll recht.* You've done well with your little ones. They are kind and precious."

Micah blinked, seeming surprised by her comment. "*Danki.* They are everything to me."

"I understand why." His comment reminded her why he needed a wife. "I told Jacob I would make him a pound cake tomorrow. I'll bring it over or send it with one of my *bruders.*"

He continued to study her as he inclined his head. "Have a *gut* night, Katie."

"Same to you, Micah."

Katie and her family arrived home by three in the afternoon. They weren't home a full hour when she heard a buggy pull into the yard. She peered through the window in time to see Jonathan Bontrager step from the vehicle and approach the house. He looked solemn, and she got the feeling that something was seriously wrong. She hurried downstairs to find out.

"Katie," Jonathan gasped as she opened the door. "We just received word that my *grossdaddi*—my *mudder*'s *dat*—fell and got hurt. We will be heading to Indiana, tomorrow. Micah wondered if you would watch the children for him."

"*Ja,* of course. I'll help in any way I can. Where are you going and when do you leave?"

"Middlebury, Indiana," Jonathan said. "First thing in the morning. We don't know what to expect. Dat wants us to come, as he may need our help with Grossdaddi's farm and my sisters with the house-hold chores."

"I'm sorry to hear to learn of your *grossdaddi*'s accident. Please tell Micah that I'll take *gut* care of his *kinner*. I can come in the morning and bring them back here."

"I'll let Micah know."

"What time will you be leaving tomorrow? I can be there as early as you need me."

"Can you come at six?"

Katie nodded. "I'll be there." Jonathan started toward his buggy. "Please tell Betty and Evan that we are thinking of them and your *grossdaddi*."

"I will. *Danki*." Then Jonathan left.

Katie's mother appeared behind her as she turned. "Was that Jonathan Bontrager?"

"*Ja*," Katie confirmed. Then she proceeded to tell her about Betty's father and the family's plans to go to Michigan. "I'll bring the children here, if it's *oll recht*."

"*Ja*. Of course." Her mother gazed out the window with concern.

"It will be fine," Katie assured her. "We will pray and everything will turn out fine."

She sent up a silent prayer that Micah's grandfather wasn't seriously hurt and for the Bontrager family.

Chapter Six

At six the next morning, Katie drove to the Evan Bontrager residence with her sister Abigail. She had planned to go by herself but wondered how she'd manage to drive home with three young children. She wasn't worried about Jacob. He was old enough to sit in the middle bench seat, but two-year-old Rebecca and one-year-old Eliza would be more of a challenge.

She glanced fondly toward her sister beside her in the front seat. Fortunately, Abigail had gotten up and finished her chores early. In fact, she and Abigail had worked together to ensure they finished everything they needed to get done. Her parents were upset to hear that Betty's father was ill, and they were more than happy to have Micah's children stay.

"I hope everything turns out *oll recht* with Betty's *dat*," Abigail said.

"*Ja*, I hope so, too." Katie worried about the family, could only imagine what they were going through. Micah must be beside himself with worrying about his grandfather and leaving his children behind to go with his parents.

The trip to Evan's property didn't take long. Katie drove onto the dirt road leading toward the residence and parked close to the barn. She and Abigail got out and started toward the house. The inside door was open, leaving only the wooden screen door to keep out bugs.

As they approached, Katie heard Micah's deep voice from inside the house as they got closer to the back door. He was having a conversation with his mother and father. She froze, unwilling to move closer, and felt her sister halt beside her.

"You don't have to come with us, Micah," Betty said. "You have a *haus* to finish and *kinner* who need you."

"Mam…"

"*Nay*, Micah," Katie heard Evan say. "We have enough help should we need it once we get to Middlebury. You stay here with your *kinner*."

"What about Katie?" Micah asked.

"She can still watch the children. How else will you be able to work on your *haus*?"

Katie exchanged concerned looks with her sister, who appeared as uncomfortable as she was.

"Hallo!" Katie called, after moving farther back in the yard after signaling her sister to do the same.

Betty came to the door, appearing glad to see her. "Come in, Katie. And Abigail? Come in! Come in!"

Katie moved first, eager to find out what everyone wanted her to do. If Micah insisted that he travel with his family to see his grandfather in Indiana, then she would continue with plans to take the children home. But what if Micah wanted to take Jacob, Rebecca and Eliza with him? *Nay*, he wouldn't do that. He was a wonderful *vadder*, and she knew it would be hard on the children to travel that far.

As soon as she stepped inside the house, she could feel the intensity of Micah's gaze. She focused her attention on Betty. "I'm sorry to hear about your *vadder*."

"*Danki*, Katie." Betty moved to the pantry and pulled out a plate of muffins, which she set on the table. "I'm glad you're here."

"*Ja*, there's been a change of plans," Micah interjected. "I'll be staying behind so rather than taking my *kinner* back to stay with you, I hope that you will feel comfortable enough to watch them here each day. Just until I get home in the afternoon after working on the *haus* renovations."

Meeting his gaze, she nodded. "I can come here. It's not a problem."

He looked relieved. *"Danki."*

"You're *willkomm*." Katie heard a vehicle pull up outside. She saw through the screened door that it was a white van, large enough to carry a big family and their belongings.

"Our ride is here," Evan said before Katie could comment. He looked at Micah. "*Soohn*, would you help us with our things?"

"*Ja*, Dat." He grabbed his parents' valises and carried them outside.

Betty and Evan left the room, and Katie could hear their footsteps on the stairs to the second floor. While Micah was absent, Emma and Addie entered the kitchen carrying small suitcases.

"Katie! Abigail!" Addie exclaimed.

"Hallo," Katie said. "I'm sorry about what happened. I'll pray for your *grossdaddi.*"

"Danki." Emma blinked back tears.

Micah entered the house and reached for his sisters' suitcases.

"I can carry mine," Emma said.

"I know you can, *schweschter.* Since I can't go with you, please let me help you."

Emma nodded, handing him her suitcase, and his sister Addie gave him hers. Micah carried their cases out to the vehicle. Jonathan, Matthew and Vernon came downstairs with their belongings.

"Katie, Abigail," Jonathan greeted with a nod before he continued outside with his suitcase.

"Matthew, Vernon, is there anything I can do to help?" Katie asked softly, noting their solemn expressions.

"Danki, Katie, but we'll be fine."

"Safe travels," Abigail said. "Katie and I will pray for your *grossdaddi.*"

Emma reentered the house. "Where are Micah's little ones?" Katie asked.

"They're still sleeping," Addie told her.

Soon everyone but the children were outside near the vehicle. Betty approached Katie where she stood with Abigail and Micah.

"Katie, *danki* for everything," she said.

"I'm glad I can help," Katie said with a soft smile. "If there is anything else I can do…"

"You're doing more than you'll ever know." Betty turned toward Micah. "We'll send word to let you know how *dei grossdaddi* is faring."

Micah nodded. His blue eyes became cloudy with worry. "Are you sure you don't want me to go?"

Evan joined his wife. "We are certain, Micah. Take care of your *kinner* and finish your *haus*. We'll look forward to seeing your progress once we get home."

The couple turned toward the large passenger van. "Mam, Dat," Micah called, drawing their attention. "Have a safe trip."

"It's in *Gott*'s hands, *soohn*," Evan said before he climbed into the vehicle after his wife and children.

Katie heard Micah huff out a breath after his family was seated in the van. As the driver drove off, Katie glanced at Micah and was immediately worried about him.

Once they were gone, Micah faced her and her sister.

"Micah," Abigail said, "would you drop me off at home?"

"Take your buggy. I'll make sure that Katie gets home safely this afternoon."

"Abigail, it would be best if you came back for me. Micah, you may be too tired to bring me when you get home." Katie looked questioningly at him. "Four thirty?" She wasn't sure it was a good idea for her to be watching the children without a vehicle should she need one. And it wouldn't be the best idea for him to take the children with him to bring her home. After Abigail had left, Katie told him about her concerns.

"I doubt after you've been working all day that you'd want the children with you when you take me home," she said. "But I don't like the idea of being without a vehicle while I'm babysitting."

Micah nodded. "Feel free to take *meim dat*'s family buggy if you need to go anywhere." His bright blue eyes gazed at her with intensity. "Do you have somewhere special you have to be?"

Katie blinked. "*Nay*, but just in case of an emergency…"

"There are other vehicles in the barn. With a family like ours, we need several carriages to get where we're going, but I'll be taking two of them to the carriage-maker's to see if any need repairs or replacement parts."

"*Oll recht. Gut* to know. I'll drive myself over tomorrow morning." She returned to the house, and he followed her inside. "What do the children like to eat for breakfast?"

Micah took her to the pantry. "This cereal is fine for all of them. Jacob will want a bowlful with milk. You can give Rebecca and Eliza some on their trays to eat with their fingers."

Katie nodded. "What about lunch?"

"There is leftover macaroni and cheese in the refrigerator. They love that, especially Jacob. But feel free to give them whatever you think is best."

The mention of Jacob made her remember her promise to him to make a pound cake. "Do you have the ingredients for a pound cake?"

His smile made her heart beat harder. "*Ja*, I'm sure my *mudder* has what you need. Help yourself. I know whatever you make will be *gut*." He ran his fingers through his hair. "I'm going to check on Jacob and then my *dechter*. I'll let you know if they are awake. I doubt they are, or we would have heard them by now, and Jacob would have come downstairs on his own."

She relaxed after Micah left the room. Why was

she so uncomfortable, so nervous suddenly? Katie looked in the pantry and pulled out the dry ingredients for a pound cake. She started to search for loaf pans in a kitchen cabinet but then stopped, debating whether it was a good time to make the cake batter.

"Nay," she murmured, "I'd better not. If the children are awake, I'll be busy feeding them." She wondered how she was going to bake with three little ones to watch over. Maybe she could find a way to entertain Jacob and the girls in the kitchen so that she could keep an eye on them while she worked.

Micah entered the room a few minutes later, carrying his sleepy son in his arms. "Jacob woke up and saw me," he explained with a soft smile for his little boy.

Katie observed, warmed by Micah's affection for his little boy. She reached for Jacob, who had been dressed by his father, but he simply burrowed against Micah's chest. She tried not to let it upset her. Jacob didn't know her well yet. Maybe once he did, he'd feel comfortable enough to let her hold him.

"I told you I'd make pound cake for you today, *ja*?"

Jacob lifted his head from his father and regarded her with bright blue eyes. He looked adorable in his little maroon short-sleeved shirt with black suspenders and navy triblend pants. His feet were bare, and she noted with a smile the boy's little toes. His father must have combed his hair, too, because his brown locks looked smooth and shiny. "You'll make pound cake?"

"Ja, I said I would, and I will. Pound cake takes time to make and then bake, but it will be ready to enjoy after lunch or supper."

Jacob struggled to get down, and Micah set his son

carefully on his feet. "Why don't you sit at the table, and Katie will get you something for breakfast." He met Katie's gaze. "I'll get the girls up and dressed."

"Are you sure I can't help? Don't you need to be over to the *haus*?"

Micah nodded toward his son. "Take care of him, and I'll bring the girls down so you can have all of them within sight before I leave. All three should sleep for you around ten until eleven or twelve."

Katie nodded. "I imagine after a busy morning they'll be tired by then."

Lips curving upward, he agreed. "I'll be right back." He left the room, leaving her a lingering awareness of him.

"Your *dat* told me that you like cereal with milk," Katie said to Jacob as she helped him into his seat by the kitchen table. She went to the pantry and pulled out a cereal box. "These?"

Jacob bobbed his head. "*Ja*, I like them. Becca and Liza does, too."

Katie took out a bowl, filled it with cereal and poured a little milk on it. "How's this?"

He smiled. "It looks *gut*."

Micah entered the room, carrying his two daughters. Both still wore their little white nightgowns. "I changed them, but as you can see, I haven't dressed them yet."

Grinning, Katie gazed at the large handsome father holding his little girls, and her heart melted. Whomever he married would be a lucky woman. Suddenly, she didn't want to envision him married to someone else.

"I'll dress them after they eat," she told him.

"Danki." He settled Eliza and Rebecca into their high chairs. "Be *gut* for Katie, *ja*?"

"We will, Dat," Jacob said.

Micah grinned at his son. *"Gut boo.* Help Katie if she needs it."

"Ja, Dat," he said before he spooned cereal with milk into his mouth then grinned as he chewed and swallowed it.

"I have to work on the new *haus,"* Micah told his son. "I'll be home later. Katie is here to take care of you."

"Where is *grossmammi* and *grossdaddi*?" the boy asked.

"They went on a trip with my *schweschters* and *bruders*."

"Why didn't we get to go?"

"Because that would make too many people in the van." He smiled at Jacob with affection. "And it's a long journey, *soohn*. Like when we moved here."

Jacob seemed to give it some thought and nodded, as if he understood. "It took too long to get here," he said.

His daughters seemed content to wait patiently for breakfast while Micah and Jacob talked.

"I'll be back this afternoon between three thirty and four. Four thirty at the latest." Micah ran a hand over his son's hair. "Will that be *oll recht*?" He reached for a glass on the table and drank the rest of his iced tea. *"Ja?"*

"Ja. Take as long as you need, Micah. Abigail will be back for me at four thirty. If you want to work longer, feel free. Abigail will wait until I'm ready to go." She studied him a moment as he checked on his children one last time before leaving. "Did you eat breakfast?" she asked.

"*Ja*, I had one of *meim mam*'s muffins."

"May I make you a sandwich for lunch?" she asked, concerned that he would skip a meal after not having much of a breakfast.

"I'll pick up something on the way," he told her, and Katie decided that from now on she would make sure that he had breakfast and lunch each day. And she would fix him supper before she headed home late this afternoon.

Micah left, and the children happily ate their cereal. Katie poured each of them a glass of milk, using sippy cups for Eliza and Rebecca so that they wouldn't spill it.

"Where's Dat?" Jacob said when he was finished breakfast.

"He is working on your new *haus*. Remember?" Katie said as she cleaned up his face and hands with a damp dish towel.

"Where's *grossmammi*?" he asked.

"She is on her way to Indiana where her *dat* lives."

Jacob blinked rapidly as if he was holding back tears. "Where's Ind-ana? I want to see them."

"Jacob, you can't right now. They will be gone for a while, but your *vadder* will be home later today." Katie watched as Jacob pushed back his chair to get down. She hurriedly helped him.

"I want Emma! I want Addie!"

"They are with your *grosseldra*."

"Why?" he wailed, his eyes filling with tears.

"Because your *grossmudder*'s *dat* is sick, and they need to help him," Katie said softly, soothingly. "But they will come home and you will see them."

He gazed up at her with eyes brimming with tears. "When?"

"I don't know. It won't be today, maybe next week, but we can have a *gut* time until they do, *ja*?"

"I want Dat!" he cried as he gazed up at her. She longed to hold and comfort him.

"He'll be home later, *oll recht*?"

Seeing their brother upset, his sisters started to cry. Katie listened to the three upset children, and she tried to think of a way to soothe them. If she could convince Jacob to calm down, maybe the girls would, too.

"Jacob, do you want to help me make pound cake?" she asked.

Sniffling, with tears on his cheeks, he looked at her with interest. "Pound cake?"

"*Ja*, with chocolate chips if you like them."

"*Ja!* I like chocolate chips!"

"Shall we go upstairs to dress your *schweschters* before we start?"

"I can help make cake?"

Katie ruffled the boy's hair. "*Ja*, you can help."

He nodded then smiled as he wiped his eyes. His sisters continued to cry. "We're going to have cake," he told them.

"Will you come upstairs with me to show me where they sleep and where their clothes are?"

He grinned. "I'm a *gut* helper. Dat says so."

"I'm sure you are."

Jacob moved toward his sisters' high chairs and began to make faces at them.

Rebecca and Eliza looked at him and they stopped crying. Their brother's antics made them laugh.

Problem solved for now! "You *are* a *gut* helper," Katie murmured with a grin. She cleaned Rebecca's face and hands then took her out of her high chair. Jacob took his sister's hand and kept her close while Katie wiped up Eliza before she picked her up. Cradling Eliza in one arm, she met Jacob's gaze. "Ready to go upstairs?" The little boy nodded. "Do you want me to carry her?" she asked, referring to Rebecca.

"I can help her," Jacob said. "I've done it before."

"*Oll recht*, let's go then."

To Katie's amazement, young Jacob was careful and considerate of his two-year-old sister as he helped her slowly up the steps to the second story. Katie had gestured for him to go ahead so that she could be close behind the two in case there was an accident and Jacob tripped and fell, pulling Rebecca with him. She was grateful that she'd had nothing to really worry about when they reached the top landing with no incident. She felt a surge of affection for Micah's children as she followed Jacob into the girls' room. Her feelings for the little ones overwhelmed her, stealing her heart. Jacob kept hold of Rebecca's hand, and Katie saw that the little girl didn't seem to mind her brother's grip.

What am I doing? These children weren't hers. She shouldn't get too attached, but how could she not? They were wonderful. She'd never have children of her own, so why not enjoy these three young ones and hope until Micah finally married and found them a new mother. Then she would have to accept the change and get over the heartbreak that was surely to come when she was no longer in their lives.

Chapter Seven

Micah stared at the existing floor in the main bed-room and debated what to install in its place. He'd had trouble concentrating since his arrival this morning. He was worried about his grandparents and concerned for his parents and siblings. And he couldn't stop thinking about Katie back at his parents' house taking care of his children.

He should be in Middlebury with his family but the trip would be too hard for Jacob, Rebecca and Eliza…and with his house… His parents had been right; it was best that he'd stayed home. He said a silent prayer for his grandfather.

He bent over to take a closer look at the wood floor. Maybe he could sand and refinish it. He'd ripped up the old vinyl in the great room downstairs and replaced it with hardwood. He loved the look of wood, especially the wider planks. The master bedroom's floor already had wide planks but it was scratched and scuffed and the finish had worn off in several places.

"*Ja*, I think I'll keep this floor and refinish it myself," he murmured. "A *gut* sanding and coat of polyurethane will make it look brand new."

His stomach growled, and he realized that he'd never picked up anything for lunch and the muffin he'd eaten for breakfast at five this morning wasn't cutting it. He glanced at his watch. It was 11:10. His children should be napping.

He wondered how Katie was making out with them. He experienced a sudden strong urge to go home for lunch. On the way back he could pick up a new battery for his power sander and sandpaper. A little "scuff" sanding to the floor would be necessary for the new finish to hold.

Once downstairs, Micah locked up the house before he climbed into his buggy and headed home. Would Katie mind if he stopped by for a quick sandwich? He surely hoped not. It wasn't a question of trusting her with his children. Because he did, as he'd told her previously. Katie was caring and warm whenever she was with them. A natural mother, he thought, and it was a shame that she had no intention of marrying and having a family.

Katie had been his late brother Jacob's betrothed. His parents had told him that Katie had grieved so much since his death that she hadn't been able to bear spending time with his family.

Micah knew what it was like after losing someone special. It had been difficult seeing his late wife's family after Anna had passed. But he'd had no choice since his children were their grandchildren. Anna's parents hadn't lived in Centreville for years. Her parents and siblings had moved during the early years

of their marriage to a very small Amish community in Idaho, outside of the town of Salmon. Apparently, the family who had first settled there were
relatives of Jeb and Marcie Miller, Anna's parents.
They had returned for Anna's funeral, and it had been
an emotional time for everyone. Later when they'd
suggested they should move back to help with the
children, Micah had assured them that he and his
offspring would be fine and that he was seriously
contemplating a move to where his family lived in
New Berne, Lancaster County, Pennsylvania. Jeb and
Marcie, who were happy in Idaho at the time, had accepted his decision to move. Micah had been grateful
for their support, he understood their concern about
seeing their grandchildren again. Micah invited them
to come for an extended visit in New Berne once he
and his children were settled in their new home.

His thoughts returned to Katie. Naomi, too, seemed
to think that Katie was still hurting. The matchmaker
had promised him that she'd keep looking for a wife
for him since Katie wasn't open to the idea. Katie was
only twenty-one. Losing Jacob had devastated her, but
he thought she was too young to know for certain that
she was done with the idea of marriage and children.
Which was why he was concerned for her.

Micah frowned as he pictured her blue eyes and
sweet face. When the Mervin Mast family had come
for Visiting Day, he'd enjoyed seeing Katie's ease and
familiarity with everyone in his family. Everyone except himself since he hadn't known her for long. It
was obvious that his parents and siblings loved Katie
and had missed having her in their lives.

His father's farm was ahead on the left. Micah turned on the battery-operated blinker on his buggy and pulled onto the property. Suddenly, he wanted to see Katie more than his need to fill his empty stomach. To ensure she was fine.

"Let's wait until your sisters are asleep before we make the cake," Katie said with a smile for Jacob. She had just put the girls down for their morning nap. "You don't need to lie down yet. You're their big *bruder*."

Jacob looked pleased. "We can make the cake while they sleep?"

Katie nodded. "We can stir all the ingredients together. Once the cake is ready for the oven, then you should lie down, too. *Ja?*"

He seemed to give it some thought. *"Oke."*

"Gut boo." She ruffled his hair. "Let's check on Rebecca and Eliza. If they are asleep, we can start on the cake."

Jacob grinned then followed her upstairs.

"You must be very quiet," Katie whispered.

He bobbed his head. *"Ja,"* he whispered back. "We can't wake 'em if they're asleep."

The girls were snoozing. Jacob was quiet as Katie tiptoed toward their beds to check on them. She smiled at Jacob as she waved him out of the room.

Once near the stairs, he said, "We can make cake now?"

Katie grinned at him. *"Ja.* Right now."

The little boy's eyes brightened. He looked so much like his father that Katie could picture a young Micah with his bright blue eyes and mop of brown hair at

Jacob's age. She thought of Micah with his blue eyes, handsome face and light brown beard that grew along his chin in the Amish way that married men wore them, and sighed. Micah was a good-looking man. He was kind and thoughtful, and the woman who married him would be grateful to have such a man in her life.

Back in the kitchen, Katie allowed Jacob to help her gather the main ingredients for the pound cake— flour, sugar, butter, eggs, baking powder, salt and vanilla extract. She found Betty's hand-crank mixer with its large bowl to stir everything together. Jacob showed her where his grandmother's loaf pans were and carried them carefully for her to the kitchen table, a flat surface he could reach easily from a chair.

Katie turned on the gas oven. While it preheated, she showed Jacob how to grease and flour the loaf pans. She carefully measured each ingredient so that he could dump them into the mixing bowl, starting with the softened butter then adding all the other ingredients. She'd decided earlier that they would make enough for two cakes—one to eat now and another to freeze for later.

Jacob grinned at her when Katie allowed him to crank the mixer.

"Carefully," Katie instructed when the little boy got a little too ambitious with his cranking. "Hold on." She scraped the sides of the bowl. "*Oll recht*, go ahead."

When the little boy got tired of turning the crank, Katie took over. Next, Katie stirred in chocolate chips by hand. Soon the cake batter was ready to be poured into the pans. Jacob watched as she tipped the bowl easily, filling each loaf pan before she placed them side by side in the preheated oven. She turned a timer on for an hour.

She turned to Jacob. "Time for a nap."

Jacob nodded. "It will be ready when I wake up?"

"It might," Katie told him. "It depends on how long you sleep. If you take a *gut* nap, it will be." She cleaned his hands and face then went with him upstairs to his room. "Sleep well, Jacob," she said as she took off his shoes. She then sat on the edge of the bed and tenderly brushed the hair off his forehead. "You were a *gut* helper today."

He grinned at her. She knew that soon at nearly four years old, Jacob would be too old for naps but not yet, as he went in for his nap willingly.

"I'll come up and check on you a little later," she told him as she stood.

"*Danki*, Katie," he murmured sleepily.

"You're *willkomm*, Jacob."

With a smile on her face, Katie went downstairs to clean up the mess from their cake making. She washed the dishes and put them away. When she finished, she decided she'd enjoy the quiet with a hot cup of tea. She put the kettle on the stove to boil then found tea bags in the cupboard. Minutes later, after settling in a kitchen chair, Katie enjoyed her first sip of the steaming brew. The morning had begun with somewhat of a rocky start, but everything had righted itself once the children had stopped crying.

Three sips into her tea, she was startled when she heard movement at the kitchen door and watched it open. Micah walked in, hung his hat on a wall hook then saw her at the table and smiled. "I hope it's *oll recht* that I'm back. I forgot to pick up something for lunch. I thought I could make a sandwich and eat here before I head back."

Katie rose, feeling her cheeks heat under his direct gaze. "I'll be happy to make you sandwich."

"No need," he said, his blue eyes crinkling at the corners as he studied her.

"Please. It will be my pleasure." She pulled her gaze from Micah, who, she realized, was far too handsome for her peace of mind. Opening the refrigerator door, she viewed its contents. "There is leftover roast beef and ham. Which one would you like?" She spoke without turning.

"Roast beef is fine," he said softly over her shoulder, making her gasp at his sudden nearness. Her heart thudded until he stepped back, giving her room.

Katie closed her eyes, drew in a calming breath and faced him. "Macaroni or potato salad with your sandwich?" she asked before she pulled out both salads from the refrigerator and set them on the countertop. Alone with him without the children, she was more aware of Micah than ever before.

"Potato salad." He reached over her head for a plate then set it on the countertop next to the salads. "I'd like a little mayonnaise on my sandwich, too, please."

Katie nodded and grabbed bread out of the pantry. She quickly made his sandwich the way he liked it, aware that he'd taken a seat at the kitchen table. After cutting the sandwich in half, she added a dollop of potato salad and set the plate with a fork on the table before him.

"What's that delicious smell?" Micah asked as he studied her.

"Pound cake. Jacob helped me make it before he went up for his nap."

He took a bite of his sandwich. Katie saw his Adam's apple bob as he swallowed. "Did you have any trouble with the children?"

"*Nay.* They were upset, at first, that you and your *grosseldra* weren't there, but they calmed down. I kept them busy during the morning, and they gave me no trouble with naptime." She checked the cake in the oven, and the wonderful scent filled the kitchen. "I'm sorry. I didn't ask. What would you like to drink? Iced tea? Lemonade?"

"Iced tea would be *gut.*"

Katie poured him cold tea from a pitcher in the refrigerator, adding two ice cubes into the glass for good measure. She then took a seat across from him to finish her hot tea. The children would be up soon, and she wanted a few quiet moments before her afternoon became busy with them. She relaxed as she cupped her tea mug and brought it to her lips. Having Micah seated across from her felt…amazingly right.

"That's probably cold by now," he said, eyeing her tea.

"It's fine." She smiled before she sipped from her tea.

He didn't say anything more for several seconds. "I appreciate your help, Katie."

"I like your *kinner.* I enjoy spending time with them." Katie thought he might say something more but then he went back to eating without a word.

Minutes went by without conversation. Strangely, she didn't feel flustered like she had earlier.

"How are the *haus* renovations coming along?" Katie asked, breaking the comfortable silence. "Did you get a lot done?"

He sighed. "I finished painting and now I'm trying to make a decision about the floors. I'll put vinyl in the children's rooms, but for the great room and master bedroom I would like to keep the wooden floors. The wood is in fine shape. I don't have much to do to it. I may use a fresh coat of a varnish or something to put some shine back. But the main bedroom's wood floor needs work. I'm thinking I'll need to sand and refinish it."

Katie got up and brought him the cookie jar filled with chocolate chip bars. She opened it and held it out to him. "Sounds nice but a lot of work."

"Ja." He grabbed a treat then took a bite. "Sanding will take a lot of time, but it will be worth it."

"My *bruder* Uri is *gut* with construction work. Maybe he can help you. Shall I ask him? Would you consider it?" Katie waited patiently for his response. She was sure her brother would agree to help Micah.

"I could use the help but…"

"Let me talk with him. I'll casually tell him about the work you're doing. If he offers to help, I'll let you know, and we can arrange to have him meet you at the *haus*." Katie took the last sip of tea, which had cooled until it was almost cold. Still, it tasted good to her.

"Katie…" Micah looked uncertain.

"I won't press him, Micah, if that's what you're afraid of." She stood and brought her mug to the sink where she filled up a dish basin with soapy water and placed it in the suds. When she turned back, he was watching her. "Is something wrong?"

"Nay," he said with a shake of his head. He finished the last cookie then stood. "I should get back to work."

"Will you still be back at 4:30?" she asked.

"Ja." He got up and brought his plate and glass to the sink. Katie reached for them, and he handed them over with a look of gratitude. "I appreciate everything you're doing for me…for us."

"It's my pleasure," Katie said, knowing that it was true. She was beginning to like Micah. A lot. It was as if she'd known him forever. He seemed more serious than his younger brother Jacob, yet she was comfortable with him after only a short time.

He grabbed his hat off the wall hook and opened the door, turning to meet her gaze. "The sandwich was delicious. *Danki*, Katie."

"You're *willkomm*, Micah." And she watched him leave with her heart pounding hard in her chest and a strange feeling enveloping her as he climbed into his buggy and, with a wave, rode off. She went back inside to the sound of the timer and pulled the two pound cakes from the oven. Katie placed them carefully on the cake racks she found earlier. She stood back and eyed them with satisfaction. The cakes were browned to perfection.

Micah wasn't gone fifteen minutes when she heard the children stirring. Jacob was talking with his sisters. As she approached the staircase, she could make out what he was saying.

"And me and Katie made chocolate chip pound cakes," he said. "It will taste so *gut*. We have to eat lunch first but then maybe each of us can have a piece."

Katie hid a smile as she climbed the stairs and entered the girls' room. "Do I hear three young *kinner* awake in here?" she said.

Jacob spun and looked up at her. "*Ja*, and we're hungry!"

"Let me change Rebecca and Eliza," Katie said, "then we'll go downstairs and eat lunch."

"And pound cake?"

She grinned at him. "*Ja*, and pound cake."

His blue eyes lit up his little face. Katie reached for Eliza first and changed her diaper before she did the same for Rebecca.

"I don't need that," Jacob said.

"Because you're a big *boo*," Katie agreed.

Carrying Micah's two young daughters, she followed Jacob down the steps. "Hold on to the bannister, Jacob," she told him.

The boy obeyed, grabbing on to the rail as he went down the stairs carefully.

Katie made the children lunch and then they each enjoyed a small piece of chocolate chip pound cake. She debated about whether she should allow Eliza a piece of cake and then decided that she would break it into bite-size pieces and see how the child did. The youngest of Micah's children loved it. By the time all of them were done eating cake, they had crumbs around their mouths and a bit of chocolate on their hands. She cleaned them up then set them down to play. By three o'clock, Eliza and Rebecca were getting sleepy so with little Jacob's help, Katie put the girls down for their afternoon nap.

It was quiet in the house after that. Katie gave Jacob a pencil and some paper. She watched as he made squiggles, which he explained were some of the animals who lived on the farm. One was a cow, another a goat and the larger one was a horse. Katie smiled at him when she heard his explanation. Jacob grinned, creating tiny dimples in his cheeks that she'd never noticed earlier. Micah's son was adorable and sweet, and she loved her time with him.

When the back kitchen doorknob rattled before opening, Katie realized how late it had gotten as Micah entered the house. She glanced at the clock. It was three forty-five. The afternoon had flown by.

"Dat!" Jacob climbed down from his chair and ran to his father.

Micah scooped up his son, making Jacob laugh and hug his father. "Have you been a *gut boo*?" he asked, meeting Katie's gaze over his son's head.

"He was a *gut* boy and a big helper today," Katie assured him.

Jacob smiled at her over his shoulder. "Katie and me made chocolate chip pound cake!"

"You did?" Lips tilting upward, Micah eyed her with approval.

"*Ja*, Dat, and it tastes delicious!" Jacob struggled to get down from his father's arms. "Come mere! I'll show you." He grabbed Micah's hand and tugged him to the pantry where Katie had stored the cake. "Look!"

Micah's expression held affection as he smiled at his son. "It looks delicious."

Jacob bobbed his head repeatedly. "It is!"

"Is this yours? Or are you going to share?"

"There's some for you, Dat. Katie made two cakes. She put one in the freezer for later."

Micah's glance immediately focused on Katie. He silently mouthed *"danki,"* and Katie could only nod and grin back at him. "Are the girls sleeping?"

"Ja, they were exhausted." Katie left the pantry to reenter the main kitchen area. Micah's presence made her stomach fluttery and caused a strange sensation to run the length of her spine. She sensed that he followed her closely. "Your *kinner* are *wunderbor,* Micah. It's a pleasure to spend time with them."

"I appreciate your time and patience with them." His expression warmed as he held her gaze. "You are a sweet and caring young woman."

Katie blushed, unused to such effusive compliments. "Have you heard from your *eldra*?"

"Nay, I don't expect to hear from them until tomorrow. It's nearly a ten-hour drive, and my *dat* wanted the driver to stop at a hotel and rest for the night."

"I hope everything is *oke* with your *grossvadder,"* she said.

"I do, too." Sounds from upstairs signaled that the girls were awake. Katie moved to get them. "I'll bring them down," Micah said. "Abigail will be here for you before you know it. I don't want to keep her waiting."

"May I make you supper? Abigail won't be here for forty-five minutes yet. I'll make something simple, an easy dish that can stay warm in the oven until you're ready to eat it."

"Katie, I don't expect you to cook for us."

"I don't mind," she said as she tied on an apron. "I enjoy cooking."

Micah grinned. "If your cooking is anything like your baking, we're all in for a treat."

Heart beating hard, Katie watched as he left the room with Jacob. Seconds later, she heard father and son go up the steps. What was easy to make that they might like? Something quick but tasty.

After digging through the refrigerator's contents, she decided to make a breakfast that was also great, in a pinch, for a supper. Made with eggs, bread, left-over ham, melted butter, milk and some cheese plus a few other minor ingredients, Katie thought Micah and his children would appreciate the hearty dish that was both filling and nutritious.

Katie quickly set the oven to 325 degrees. She assembled the ingredients then placed the mixture into an oblong pan. When he appeared with a daughter in each arm ten minutes later, he was surprised to see her slide the casserole into the oven and set a timer for forty-five minutes.

"I made a breakfast casserole," she explained. "I'll be happy to have something else ready when you get home tomorrow, but this was quick and easy and…" She blushed. "I hope you like breakfast casserole. I used the leftover ham."

"I love breakfast casserole and so do my *kinner*," he said, appearing stunned yet pleased that she'd gone to the trouble.

"When the timer goes off, just turn down the heat and leave the dish in the oven to keep warm until you're ready to eat it." The sound of buggy wheels filtered in through the screened door. "That must be my *schweschter*. She's a little early." She quickly set the table for them for later. "What time should I be back in the morning? Six?"

"No need to come then. Eight is fine. Or you can come at nine if you'd like." He put down Rebecca. "Katie, I can set a table."

She looked at him. "I know." Was he upset with her? *Nay*, he wouldn't be smiling if he was. She returned his smile. "I'll be here at eight tomorrow. Have a nice night, Micah." Katie turned her attention to his son. "I'll see you tomorrow, Jacob." She picked up Rebecca and gave the child a hug before setting her down again. Eliza reached for Katie from her father's arms. Instead of taking her, she gently caught the child's hand and smiled at her. "See you soon," she whispered.

With a nod in Micah's direction, Katie left, aware that he had followed her into the yard, holding both daughters again. She waved, pleased when he waved back at her.

"Looks like you had a *wunderbor* day," Abigail said as she pulled the vehicle onto the road in the direction of home.

"I enjoyed myself," Katie admitted. "The children were so *gut*, and… I…liked spending time with them."

"So, you don't mind going back tomorrow?"

"*Nay*, not at all." Katie thought of Micah and knew her eagerness to return was due not only to her enjoyment of the children, but because she'd get to see their father again.

Chapter Eight

The next morning Katie steered the horse-drawn buggy toward the Bontrager residence, her thoughts on her conversation with her mother the night before.

How was it? Mam had asked as they'd worked side by side, preparing a light meal for the family.

Gut. *The children are* wunderbor. *I enjoyed watching them. Jacob helped me make chocolate chip pound cake. I let him add all the measured ingredients, and he loved it. His blue eyes lit up when I allowed him to take a turn stirring.*

Her mother had smiled. *That's nice that you included him.*

It was fun, and Jacob is easy to please. Katie had fried bacon in a cast-iron pan as they chatted. *They're having breakfast casserole*, she said with a grin. *I made it for Micah and the children before I left.*

Mam had paused in the act of taking out dinner plates. *You cooked for them*, she said, nodding in approval. She set the plates on the table and returned to pull out two oblong baking dishes. *Katie, you don't*

have to be home in time to prepare supper with me.
Your sisters can help. If Micah and the children need
a meal, do what you can for them. If Micah happens
to invite you to eat with them, stay.

"*Mam...*"

Katie, I'm not asking you to marry the man. I'm
simply saying it's gut *that you help him whenever*
you can. I saw Naomi earlier today and she's ac-
tively looking for a wife for him. Until then, he needs
someone to watch his children and cook his meals if
he doesn't have time.

As a car passed her on her way to the Bontrager
farm, Katie continued to think about her mother's
words. Her involvement in their lives was a temporary situation. *Mam is right. I should help Micah and*
the children whenever I can.

"Naomi *is* actively seeking a wife for him," she
murmured as she tried not to visualize Micah with
another woman. Why did the fact that he would eventually marry someone else bother her? *Because I'm*
worried about his kinner. She knew instinctively that
it wasn't the only reason she was upset. She shouldn't
be since she'd already decided not to marry or have a
family. She should be happy for Micah when Naomi
finally found him a wife and mother for his children. Katie thought of Jacob with his adorable smile
and Rebecca who grinned at her as she ate whatever Katie put in front of her. And little Eliza… She
would miss her tiny hugs, the way her body would
curl against her in sleep or when she held on. Micah's
new wife would feed his children, put them down for

their naps…and be with Micah after the sun went down and the children were in bed.

Katie felt her throat tighten as the Bontrager property loomed ahead. She parked near the barn and headed toward the house. The door opened at her approach. Micah stood there, looking too handsome for her tranquility of mind in a royal blue short-sleeved shirt and navy triblend trousers held up by dark suspenders. As she closed the distance between them, the man flashed her a smile.

"*Gut* morning, Katie," he murmured, the sound of his deep, pleasant voice vibrating down her spine.

"*Hallo*, Micah. Is that your wagon?" she said, jerking her head toward the vehicle and noticing the family buggy parked beside the barn. She hoped the wagon didn't belong to Naomi because it meant the matchmaker had come with news of a potential match for him.

"*Nay, meim vadder*'s. I need it to pick up vinyl flooring this morning for the children's rooms."

Relieved, Katie nodded. "Did you eat breakfast?"

"I did. *Danki.* I reheated some of the tasty breakfast casserole you made us for last night's supper." He held the door open for her, and she was aware of his clean masculine scent—of soap and time spent outdoors in the fresh air—as she passed by him to enter the house. Every one of her senses buzzed with awareness.

"I'm glad you enjoyed it," she said, stunned by her reaction.

"The children loved it. I warmed it in the oven for ten minutes. Eliza's messy fingers as she popped bite-size pieces into her mouth told me how much she enjoyed it."

Katie laughed. "That's *gut*." She saw that his daughters were happy in their high chairs. "Why don't you let me make you lunch?"

When she met his gaze, she found that he watched her intently.

"You don't have to—"

"Micah, I'm happy to do that for you. I see that you already dressed the children. I don't mind dressing them each morning. I'm sure you have enough to do to get ready for work. Let me see what's in the refrigerator for your lunch." She noticed the coffee-pot on the stove as she moved to check on the food. She paused. "Would you like a cup of coffee while you wait?"

"*Ja*, I would. *Danki*. It should still be hot."

Katie poured him a cup of coffee and set it before him with sugar. She reached into the refrigerator for a jug of milk and placed it on the table within his reach.

She made him a sandwich of cold roast beef and cheddar cheese, put the sandwich in a paper lunch bag and added a wrapped piece of pound cake. When she turned around, Micah was sipping from his coffee mug, watching her. "A sandwich and cake," she said. "Would you like iced tea in a thermos?"

He nodded. *"Danki."*

Katie found the thermos she'd seen the day before in a cabinet when she was looking for loaf pans. She filled it to the brim with the tea, sealed it and added the outer cup lid. "Here you go," she said with a smile, placing it on the table near him.

"I appreciate this." He stood then grabbed the thermos and bag. "I'll be home between four and four thirty."

"Take your time. I'll fix supper for you."

"Katie, that doesn't seem fair."

"I like to cook, Micah. Is there anything you don't like?"

He shook his head. "I can't think of anything." He grabbed his hat, opened the door and settled the hat on his head. Once outside, he faced her. "I'll see you later. Maybe tomorrow we can arrange for you to come with the children to the *haus*. I'd like your opinion about the interior."

Katie nodded. "*Oll recht.* Just let me know when." She watched him put his lunch in the back before he climbed onto the seat. "Have a nice day!"

He smiled and waved, and Katie quickly turned back to the children who were eagerly waiting to get down from their high chairs and the table. She cleaned up their hands and faces and helped them from their chairs. "Would you like to play outside for a while?" she asked Micah's son.

"Ja!" Jacob exclaimed. "Can we eat a picnic outside?"

"We can, but not today," Katie said, grinning. "Maybe tomorrow. It is important that you stay in the backyard and near me. *Ja?*"

The little boy bobbed his head eagerly.

"Wait here a moment so I can see what's in the freezer for supper. Your *dat* can't be here for a midday meal so I'll make something *gut* for all of you for dinner." She looked in the freezer and saw a pack of chicken. She could make fried chicken and mashed potatoes, she thought as she pulled out the chicken and placed it in the refrigerator. She'd place it in warm water to thaw it later while the children napped.

Katie searched in a chest of drawers in the great room and found a quilt that looked as if it had been used outside in the past as a picnic blanket. *I'll wash it once we are done outside.* Throwing the quilt over her arm, she went into the kitchen to see Jacob standing near the back door with a wide grin on his face.

She eyed Jacob's hands. "Are your hands clean?"

The boy bobbed his head. "I wiped them *gut.*"

"*Wunderbor.* Let's bring out paper and a pencil. You can find things in the backyard to draw."

She found paper and pencil where she'd put it yesterday. She gave them to Jacob and grabbed a kitchen cutting board for him to use as a lap desk.

Katie turned her attention to Micah's daughters. She wiped their faces and hands then lifted Rebecca down from her chair before reaching for Eliza. After picking up the little girl, she held the child close to her and reached for Rebecca's hand.

It was a beautiful day. The sun shone on the dew-covered lawn. Katie debated where to put the quilt because of the dampness on the ground but decided it didn't matter. The quilt was thick enough to keep them dry. With Jacob's help, she managed to spread out the quilt then ensured that each child stayed close to her. It was nice for them all to get some fresh air.

The morning went quickly. Jacob was content to

draw, and Katie was able to keep the two younger children entertained. Before she knew it, it was time for Rebecca and Eliza to nap. To her amusement, the fresh air had made Jacob quiet.

"Let's go inside, Jacob." She stood up, reached for the two little girls. Jacob got up silently with his pencil and papers.

The interior house was dark compared to the bright outside, but her eyes adjusted quickly. Within minutes, she had them upstairs in their beds. Their eyes closed immediately, and it didn't take long for the three of them to fall asleep. Katie made bread while they slept. Once she had put two loaves in the oven, she placed the frozen chicken in warm water to thaw then fixed herself a cup of tea and sat down to relax.

When she pulled the bread out of the oven an hour later, she realized it was lunchtime. She searched in the pantry for something to make the children to eat after they woke up. There were jars of homemade jams and jellies in several flavors. Katie checked the refrigerator and found a few flavors already open. She'd make them jam sandwiches—or peanut butter and jelly. Most children, including her siblings when they were young, loved peanut butter and jelly. She smiled as she left the kitchen and headed toward the stairs to check on the children.

The house held the aroma of fresh bread as she climbed the steps. She heard noise from Jacob's room and entered to find him awake, sitting on the floor with a marble roller. She watched him place a marble on the wooden track and smiled at his delight as it rolled from the top to the bottom.

"Jacob."

He blinked as he looked up at her. "I woke up."

She nodded, hiding her amusement. "I see that." She paused as he scrambled to his feet. "Please pick up your toy and put it where no one can trip over it."

Katie smiled in approval as he quickly obeyed. "Shall we check on your sisters?"

"*Ja.* I'm sure they're hungry, too," he said as he followed her out of the room.

"Would you like a peanut butter and jelly sandwich for lunch?"

His grin melted her heart. "I like peanut butter and jelly."

They entered the girls' room just as Eliza stirred. Rebecca was already awake. She carried the girls downstairs and fixed them lunch. All three of the children were in good spirits. The afternoon went quickly with the girls napping. Jacob sat at the kitchen playing with the marble roller she'd retrieved from his room while Katie took the chicken out of the refrigerator where she'd put it after it thawed. It was close to four in the afternoon. Micah would be home at any time.

Satisfied that Jacob was happily occupied, she breaded the chicken and set it aside until it was time to fry it. By the time that Micah came home, his dinner of fried chicken, mashed potatoes and chowchow would be ready for him. She looked forward to seeing his enjoyment of the meal. The thought of seeing him made her smile, and she felt the tiny twinge of excitement in knowing that he could walk in the door at any time.

Get ready to relax and indulge with your FREE BOOKS and more!

Claim up to FOUR NEW BOOKS & TWO MYSTERY GIFTS – absolutely FREE!

Dear Reader,

We both know life can be difficult at times. That's why it's important to treat yourself so you can relax and recharge once in a while.

And I'd like to help you do this by sending you this amazing offer of up to FOUR brand new full length FREE BOOKS that WE pay for.

This is everything I have ready to send to you right now:

Try **Love Inspired® Romance Larger-Print** books and fall in love with inspirational romances that take you on an uplifting journey of faith, forgiveness and hope.

Try **Love Inspired® Suspense Larger-Print** books where courage and optimism unite in stories of faith and love in the face of danger.

Or **TRY BOTH!**

All we ask in return is that you answer 4 simple questions on the attached Treat Yourself survey. You'll get **Two Free Books** and **Two Mystery Gifts** from each series you try, *altogether worth over $20*! Who could pass up a deal like that?

Sincerely,

Pam Powers

Harlequin Reader Service

Treat Yourself to Free Books and Free Gifts.

Answer 4 fun questions and get rewarded.

► DETACH AND MAIL CARD TODAY! ►

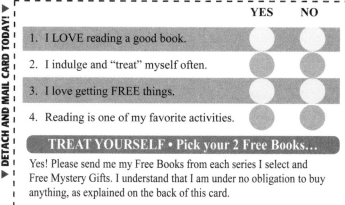

	YES	NO
1. I LOVE reading a good book.	○	○
2. I indulge and "treat" myself often.	○	○
3. I love getting FREE things.	○	○
4. Reading is one of my favorite activities.	○	○

TREAT YOURSELF • Pick your 2 Free Books...

Yes! Please send me my Free Books from each series I select and Free Mystery Gifts. I understand that I am under no obligation to buy anything, as explained on the back of this card.

Which do you prefer?

❏ **Love Inspired® Romance Larger-Print** 122/322 IDL GRDP
❏ **Love Inspired® Suspense Larger-Print** 107/307 IDL GRDP
❏ **Try Both** 122/322 & 107/307 IDL GRED

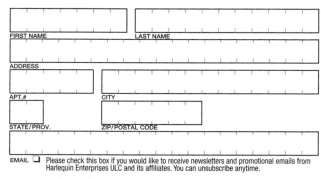

FIRST NAME | LAST NAME

ADDRESS

APT.# | CITY

STATE/PROV. | ZIP/POSTAL CODE

EMAIL ❏ Please check this box if you would like to receive newsletters and promotional emails from Harlequin Enterprises ULC and its affiliates. You can unsubscribe anytime.

© 2022 HARLEQUIN ENTERPRISES ULC
™ and ® are trademarks owned by Harlequin Enterprises ULC. Printed in the U.S.A.

LI/SLI-520-TY22

* * *

Micah moved his tools into the master bedroom before leaving and locking the house. As he drove his wagon home, he wondered what Katie was making for dinner. She'd been a lifeline for him. Her kindness, compassion and warmth when dealing with his children made him appreciate her even more. He knew that Naomi was looking for a wife for him, but he found that he wasn't in any hurry to meet someone new, not with Katie there ready to step in and help. But was it fair for him to expect her to take care of his children? Of him?

It was a short trip home. As soon as he entered the house, he was hit with the tantalizing aroma of food. Fresh bread. Fried chicken. He hung up his hat and looked for her.

Katie was at the stove flipping chicken over in a fry pan. She turned at the sound of the door. Her smile warmed him. "You're home."

Jacob looked up from his drawing. "Dat!" He pushed back his chair, got down and ran to him. Micah felt overwhelming love for his son as Jacob hugged him with his little arms around Micah's legs. As he held the boy against him, he spied his two daughters who were content in their high chairs.

"How were they?" he asked Katie.

"*Gut.* We had a nice day."

Jacob pulled back to gaze up at his father. "I was a *gut boo.* I had two naps and I helped Katie."

Micah settled his gaze on the young woman, who nodded with a look of affection for Jacob. He liked seeing Katie in his parents' home. Her face was flushed from the heat of the stove. A tiny strand of blond hair had come undone at the right side of her forehead. Her blue eyes sparkled with pleasure until something in her expression changed as their gazes continued to stay locked, and she looked suddenly guarded.

He moved farther into the room. "Something smells delicious."

"Fried chicken, mashed potatoes and fresh bread. I looked for fresh green beans in your *mudder*'s garden but couldn't find any left. I found a jar of chow-chow in the refrigerator I thought you might enjoy instead." She seemed to relax a little as she discussed supper. "The chicken will be done in a minute or two." She flipped the pieces of chicken in the skillet as she spoke. "Do you think that Eliza will be able to eat any of this food? If not, I can cook something else for her."

"She'll be fine with everything you made."

Katie grinned. "I'm happy to hear that."

Micah saw that she had set the table earlier, but several plates had been pushed to one side so that Jacob had a place to draw. He addressed his son. "Want to show me what you drew?"

He watched the child run to the table and pick up a several sheets of paper, which he brought back to show him.

"This one is a tree, like the one out back."

He eyed Jacob's pencil drawing and smiled. "That's a *gut* drawing, *soohn*."

"And this one is us." There were five stick figures

without faces. "This one is you, Dat. These are me, Becca and Eliza. And that one is Katie."

Micah froze. "Nice," he said, but inside his heart was hammering hard. Why would he draw Katie with the rest of them?

"Katie is with us, because she is like family 'cuz she helps us," Jacob explained with a young child's innocence.

"I see." He glanced toward Katie and was grateful that she hadn't heard what Jacob had said. At least, he didn't think she had. She was intent on cooking, and he saw no change in her demeanor, no tension in her shoulders.

He watched her take the chicken out of the skillet and place it on a plate with paper towels to drain the pieces. She lifted the lid of a pot and stirred its contents. *Mashed potatoes.*

Within minutes, Katie had them all seated at the table before she brought over their food. A loaf of bread came first, sliced into mouthwatering pieces, followed by the butter dish. She put out a bowl of his mother's sweet chow-chow. Next, she set out a platter of fried chicken that smelled wonderful and looked even better along with a bowl of mashed potatoes, and the meal was complete.

"I hope you enjoy it," she said as she untied her apron as if to get ready to leave.

"Katie, stay. Sit down and eat with us." He could see indecision on her pretty features. *"Sigh so gude."* Please.

"If you're sure you don't mind…" she began.

"Eat with us, Katie!" Jacob urged.

She looked at Jacob before meeting Micah's gaze. "Micah."

"I won't force you to eat with us, but we'd like you to stay. *Ja, soohn?*"

"*Ja*, Dat!"

Micah was rewarded with her smile.

"*Danki.*" She pulled out a chair and sat down. "*Ach nay!* Drinks! What would you like to drink?" She started to rise, but Micah placed his hand on her arm, stopping her.

"I'll get the drinks." She looked stunned by his offer and he hid a smile. "Jacob, milk? Katie? Iced tea or would you like something else?"

She blinked. "Iced tea is fine."

He nodded. Micah poured milk for the children and iced tea for Katie and himself. When he sat back in his seat, he saw Katie eye him curiously but with a softness in her expression that made him inhale sharply.

He realized that he enjoyed spending time with Katie Mast way too much. *We are friends. Nothing more.* It was only natural for Katie to eat with them since she'd worked so hard to prepare a delicious meal.

The image of his wife Anna's face slipped into his mind, but he forced it away. It wasn't wrong to eat dinner with Katie, who cared for his children while he worked. It wasn't wrong. Memories of his life with Anna rose to haunt him. Guilt hit him hard, but he refused to allow it to ruin their lovely meal—or his friendship with Katie Mast.

Chapter Nine

Micah couldn't stop thinking about Katie. She'd been taking care of his children daily for four days, and something about her lingered in his mind. It felt wrong to develop feelings for her. He had loved his wife, Anna, and it didn't seem right to care for another woman with Anna not in her grave a full year, but his feelings for Katie were complicated and constantly growing.

I need to fight feeling for Katie the way I do. I know I must marry again, and I thought I wanted a wife who will be happy with simply caring for my children. Like a marriage of convenience or a business arrangement. Whenever he thought of marrying again, he pictured Katie in his life, in his home, as a mother to his children. And there was nothing convenient about that.

He and Katie enjoyed a friendship. Katie had loved Jacob and still did. He realized he must find a way to distance himself mentally and physically to fight his growing feelings for her. And he needed to do it now, because he knew she wasn't ready, may never be ready to move on.

Micah got down on his knees and scuff-sanded the bedroom floor, smoothing out the scratches and nicks with the sandpaper. He worked vigorously, spurred on by his dilemma because of Katie and his confusing thoughts.

Each night Katie continued to cook for him, and they enjoyed supper together with the children like a family. Micah had realized he was in big trouble when he found himself frequently heading home for lunch so that he could spend more time with her. He couldn't continue this way. Something had to change before he said something to Katie that he'd regret.

Naomi, his matchmaker, needed to find a wife for him and soon. Katie was off-limits, because she was having a hard time forgetting his deceased brother, the man she'd loved.

He sanded the floor harder, running it from one side of the room to the other. He shouldn't be working so hard to get the house done, because if the matchmaker hadn't found him a spouse once he finished, Katie would be here in his house, watching his children, while he worked on building a new outbuilding on his farm. Seeing Katie in his house would be difficult, giving him ideas of a happily ever with her that would never come true. He had loved Anna. It felt disloyal to think of Katie as anything other than his brother Jacob's girl, but Micah couldn't help himself. He knew that if she ever learned how he felt, she'd avoid him. Could he deal with her rejection? *Nay*, so he would have to keep his feelings private, pretend that every moment in her company wasn't hurting his heart.

Micah rose, surveyed his handiwork and winced. Lost in thought, he'd gotten a little too ambitious in one part of the room. He would have to figure out a way to make the uneven sanded surfaces of the wood flow together with the finish. The idea of going home for lunch pleased him, but he knew it wouldn't be wise, given his current feelings. He decided that he would stay and work until noon then run over to Kings for a sandwich. And he'd eat lunch here in the house and force himself to concentrate on what he needed to do next rather than ponder his growing affection for Katie.

Katie fed the children and tried her best to smile at the little ones who had no idea that she was upset Micah hadn't come home for lunch. He and she had enjoyed sharing both lunch and dinner these last two days. But he seemed different this morning. Quieter.

Was he worried about the house renovations? He hadn't confided in her. He'd seemed distant—a distance that bothered her more than it should.

As she continued with her day, Katie fought to convince herself that Micah's behavior didn't concern her. After all, she wasn't marrying the man. *Nay*, he'd be marrying someone else, a woman Naomi found for him, and she had no right to feel slighted. She was just the babysitter. With the firm reminder of her position, Katie washed the clothes she gathered from the upstairs bedrooms earlier as Rebecca and Eliza slept. Next, she planned supper while Jacob played quietly at the kitchen table until, bored, he climbed down and stood by her side.

"What'cha doing?" he asked.

"Making macaroni and cheese for your supper."

The little boy beamed at her. "I love mac'roni and cheese!"

She gave him an affectionate smile. "Why don't you play in the great room until your sisters wake up, *ja*?"

"Oke." He obeyed and left the room. She looked in on him a few minutes later and found his attention occupied by two wooden toys: a horse with wheels and what looked like a farm tractor.

"Jacob? Let me know if you hear your sisters, *ja*? Or you can come and play in the kitchen, and we'll check on them in a little while."

"I'll play here," he told her, preoccupied with his toys. "If I hear them, I'll tell you."

Katie smiled and thanked him before she returned to the kitchen.

The macaroni and cheese casserole was a simple and easy meal to make. The girls woke up shortly after she'd placed the casserole to keep in the refrigerator until it was time to put it in the oven. She brought Rebecca and Eliza downstairs.

"Feel like a snack?" she asked Jacob as she stopped with a sister in each arm.

"Cake?" He looked hopeful.

"How about crackers with cheese?"

"Oke."

The rested girls were in good humor as she took them into the kitchen where she set each one in her high chair. Jacob followed them and took his seat at the table. Katie gave each of them a small cup of milk and a light snack of cheese and crackers to hold them over until supper.

Two hours later Katie pulled the hot, bubbling cheese dish out of the oven as Micah entered the house. "Something smells *gut*," he said pleasantly.

She set the hot dish on top of the stove before she faced him. He offered her a smile that was less than his usual good-humored one, and it struck Katie again that something was bothering him.

"It's just macaroni and cheese," she told him as she busied herself pulling out plates, utensils and napkins. "Supper will be but a minute," she said, setting the table for him and Jacob.

She would make sure everything was ready, then she would leave. If he asked her to stay, then she would know she wasn't the reason he was so distant, that whatever was bothering him wasn't because of something she'd done. She shot him a glance, caught his frown as he eyed the table. He was so handsome that he stole her breath. He was Jacob's older brother, and she'd never expected to feel this strongly for him.

"I'll get your drinks ready," she said, "and then I'll leave you to eat." She managed a smile for him. "I know it's not much of a meal. I took the other pound cake out of the freezer. I saw vanilla ice cream in there if you'd like to have it with your cake." She knew she was babbling. "Iced tea?" She saw him nod. She pulled out a tall glass for him and small plastic cups for the children. "I thought the children should have milk again. Unless you'd like them to have something else to drink." When he didn't respond, she found herself blinking back tears. *I will not cry.* She composed herself as she fixed their drinks and placed them within easy reach of Micah's family. "Do you need anything else?"

"Katie." Micah's deep voice drew her attention to him.

"Ja?" She gazed up at him with a suddenly tight throat.

"Why aren't you staying to eat with us?"

"I don't know if that's a *gut* idea," she whispered, looking away.

He was silent, but she could feel him watching her. "Katie—"

His tone drew her gaze to him. *"Ja?"* Her heart beat hard. Something in his expression alerted her that she wasn't going to like what he had to say.

"I was finally able to talk with my *dat* on the phone this morning. My *grossvadder* is doing much better. My *eldra* are hoping to head home any day now. I'm taking tomorrow off, so I won't need you to watch my *kinner.*" He averted his eyes.

"Oll recht," she said softly, her heart hurting. "There are leftovers in the refrigerator. You should have enough to eat for the next day or so. If you need anything, send word and I'll see what I can do to help." She untied her apron. "Enjoy your supper, Micah."

Katie turned quickly away to hang up the apron. She didn't want him to see that she was upset that he was fine with her leaving. It was always a given that her time with them would end. Katie just hadn't expected it to be this soon. Nor had she expected to feel this heartache.

She smiled at him and then headed toward the door.

"Katie?"

Katie spun to face him.

"Danki," he said softly.

She nodded. "You're *willkomm*, Micah." Feeling the oncoming threat of tears, she quickly opened the door and left.

Katie allowed herself to cry as she drove home. Spending time with Micah and his children made her realize what she would never have. *Jacob, why did you have to die?* She sent up a silent prayer for help. *Gott, help me be content with my decision to stay single.* After caring for the family, she suddenly was having a hard time with her choice.

Once home, she headed inside to help her mother with supper. She'd spent only a few days with Micah and his young ones but that short time with them had changed her forever.

"Katie!" Her mother's eyes widened as Katie entered the house. "I thought you'd be eating with Micah and the children."

She managed a smile. "*Nay*, I fixed their supper and left. Micah won't be working tomorrow so I'll be able to get back to sewing. I still have Lucy Fisher's mending to do."

Katie could feel her mother's concerned gaze on her as she set the table.

"Is something wrong?" Mam asked.

She shook her head, dismissing her mother's worry. "What could be wrong?"

"*Dochter...*"

"I'm fine, Mam. Micah doesn't need me now, and it's fine."

Her mother studied her a long moment. "Would you peel the potatoes?"

Nodding, Katie went right to work. She would

keep busy and wait until, or if, Micah needed her again. If he didn't, that would be fine. She had a sewing business to get off the ground. Besides Lucy's mending to do, she needed to make aprons, prayer *kapps* and items that visiting Englishers might like for her to sell at Kings General Store.

The next morning Katie arose early and it occurred to her with a start that there was no reason for her to head toward the Bontrager residence to take care of Micah's children. Disappointment overwhelmed her as she went downstairs to help her mother and sisters with breakfast. After she ate with her family, she returned to her bedroom, where she pulled fabric out of a dresser drawer. She then got to work on the sewing machine that was set up in her room. She concentrated on sewing, only taking a break for the midday meal and later for supper before she went back to work.

That night Katie fell into bed, tired from all the hours of work she'd done. She was too exhausted to think about Micah and the children until she woke up in the middle of the night and thoughts of them returned, causing her to worry about what she'd done so terribly wrong that Micah no longer wanted her around.

By the time the morning sunshine filtered in through her curtains, Katie had slept only a few hours, and she felt groggy with sleep. After coffee with breakfast, she started her day as she had begun yesterday with sewing and mending until late afternoon when she was finally finished with the work she'd wanted done.

She'd make her deliveries tomorrow morning, Katie decided. That night when she went to bed, she had trouble falling asleep. She was plagued with images of Micah—and Jacob, her late betrothed. She stared at the ceiling and blinked back tears. She missed Micah and the children. The knowledge that she missed Micah made her feel guilty, as if she was betraying Jacob's memory. But she couldn't stop caring about Micah and his little ones.

It was best that Micah no longer needed her, she thought the next morning as she packed up items to be delivered to the store and to Lucy Fisher. *I miss Micah's children, because I won't be having any of my own.* Katie had always wanted to be a wife and mother, but God had planned another life for her when He'd called Jacob home.

As she carried her delivery items to her pony cart, Katie saw that the day was a little overcast with the sun peeking in and out from behind the clouds. Good weather for being out and about making deliveries.

She drove to Kings General Store and dropped off the items for sale she'd promised Rachel King during the last church service day.

Rachel greeted her with a smile as Katie entered the shop, stirring the bells on the door. "Our customers are going to love these," she said as she held up an apron from the box of items that Katie had brought. Her eyes widened as she saw the white organza Amish prayer *kapps*. "You did a *wunderbor* job with the head coverings. Not everyone can make them. These *kapps* will sell out in no time."

"*Danki*, Rachel. I'm happy that you're willing to help me out this way," Katie told her. "If anyone mentions they need someone to do mending, would you give out my name?"

"*Ja*, of course! Do you have a cell phone?" Rachel asked.

"*Nay*, I…my *vadder* doesn't think they are necessary."

"I'm sure the church elders will approve one for business use. Explain to your *dat* and see what he says first."

Katie nodded. She glanced outside and saw dark clouds gathering in the distance. "Is it supposed to rain?"

"*Ja*. There is a chance of a severe thunderstorm but not until this afternoon," Rachel said. "Would you like some tea?"

"*Nay*, but *danki*. I have one last delivery for Lucy Fisher. Another day?"

Rachel smiled. "*Ja*. You are always *willkomm*. Tell Lucy *hallo* from me." Her expression was soft. "Her first baby with Gabriel. The two of them must be thrilled. Gabriel loves her first two like his own. Still, I love to see them so happy as they extend their family."

Katie nodded. "*Ja*. They are *wunderbor eldra*. Is it *oke* if I bring more items in a few weeks?"

"*Ja*. Anything you make we'll take." Rachel laughed. "I'll let you know what sells the quickest, although I'm sure everything you brought in will sell. You are truly a skilled seamstress." She picked up the box that Katie had brought in. "Enjoy your day, Katie. Stop by anytime."

With a wave and smile, Katie left for Gabriel Fisher's house with the basket of finished mending that Lucy had hired her to do.

Lucy opened the door as Katie stepped down from her vehicle. She grabbed Lucy's basket and headed toward the house. "*Gut mariga*, Lucy!" she called out with a wave. She could see Lucy's wide smile as Katie drew closer.

"*Gut* morning to you, Katie! Want to stay awhile and chat?" Lucy said as Katie carried the basket into the house.

After a quick glance at her wristwatch, Katie saw that there was time. She smiled. "I'd like that."

"Coffee or tea?"

"What would you prefer?" Katie asked, unwilling to have Lucy wait on her.

"Iced tea."

"Do you have enough made?" When Lucy nodded, Katie insisted on waiting on Lucy. "How are you feeling?" she asked.

"I'm feeling *gut*." Lucy took a sip of the iced tea. "You stopped by at the perfect time. Susie is with Gabriel in his workshop. Our *soohn* is napping."

"I'm glad I came at the right time," Katie said.

The two women drank iced tea and caught up.

"I heard you were helping Micah Bontrager with the children." Lucy settled a hand on her pregnant belly.

"*Ja.* It's been a pleasure to spend time with his little ones. Betty's *vadder* is ill, and the family left for Indiana to see what they could do to help. Micah stayed home—at his *dat*'s insistence—to be there for his children when he's not working on the *haus*. The journey would have been too much for them anyway."

Katie didn't want to talk about Micah or the children, but Lucy's gentle manner made it easier to discuss the subject. She was relieved that Lucy didn't ask any uncomfortable questions about Micah, perhaps because Lucy knew how devastated Katie was by Jacob's death.

They discussed many things including Lucy's pregnancy and her husband, Gabriel. They talked about Katie's sewing, about recipes they liked, which they shared, until Katie realized how late it was.

"Danki," Katie said as she picked up their glasses and washed them at the sink.

"You don't have to do that!" Lucy moved to help, grabbing a dishtowel to dry the glasses.

"Take the help when you can get it," Katie teased.

"Gabriel helps me a lot."

Katie softened her expression. "I know he does. You married a *gut* man, Lucy Fisher."

"Ja, I'm extremely fortunate to have him."

The sky had darkened by the time Katie climbed into her buggy to return home. She realized that she had stayed at Lucy's too long, but it was nice to spend time with her friend. Lucy was fortunate in her second marriage. She'd found a new love in Gabriel Fisher, a man much more generous and loving than Lucy's first husband, Harley, who hadn't been interested in his new spouse after the death of his beloved first wife. *Which is why people who have loved and lost should not marry if they aren't able to accept them as they should.*

Thunder rumbled in the distance as she drove toward home. The darkened sky was expanding, and a streak of lightening lit up the clouds startling her, making her cry out. The initial rain became a downpour as the storm roared in with a vengeance. Katie knew she needed to find shelter in the worsening storm. She steered her buggy, keeping to the side of the road, concerned with her horse which she feared would spook if she didn't get her inside soon.

It was too far for her to go home. A property loomed ahead in the near distance, and Katie recognized it as the Evan Bontrager residence. *I can't stop there.* She hadn't seen Micah in two days. It would be awkward, and she didn't want to come across as needy.

The next lightning flash followed by a horrendous boom of thunder had her rethinking her decision to keep going until she found another place to get out of the rain. She steered her vehicle onto the Bontrager property and parked near the barn. There were no other buggies in the barnyard. It was entirely possible that Micah and the children weren't home. She ran to the rear door first and knocked hard but no one answered.

Katie raced back to the barn and opened it. If she could find an empty stall...

There was one close to the door. She unhitched her mare from the cart and brought the animal inside to the dry, empty stable. Satisfied that her horse would settle and be safe, she walked the length of the outbuilding as she searched for another place for her to sit. There were no other stalls available. She went back to her horse and sat outside the stall door. When the storm raged loudly, making her scared more than nervous, she slipped inside the stall and took refuge in a back corner. Hugging herself with her arms, Katie prayed that the storm would be over soon so that she could go home and take comfort in the company of her family.

Chapter Ten

"Jacob, stay by my side," Micah said as he walked down an aisle in Kings General Store. His youngest daughter, Eliza, sat in the seat of the shopping cart. Rebecca was being entertained by Rachel King behind the counter in the back of the store. She'd offered to take Eliza, too, but he thought he could manage Eliza and find the grocery items he needed for the next couple of days. Meals he could fix easily.

"Dat, can I have a cookie?"

"We have cookies at home," Micah said.

"A cupcake?" Jacob looked up at him, his eyes filled with hope and innocence.

"*Ja*, maybe a cupcake, but only if you help me shop like the *gut boo* you are."

His son beamed up at him with excitement. "What do we need next, Dat?"

Micah ruffled Jacob's hair as he regarded him with affection. He loved his children. They were his world. Which was why he was willing to marry again—not because he needed a wife but because his children needed a mother.

The image of Katie filled his mind, creating an ache in his heart, as he pushed the cart down the aisle. There had been something about her from the first moment they'd met that captured his attention. But then when he learned that she'd been his younger brother's betrothed...

She will never marry. He could see her married and with children. *With me.* His own thoughts shocked him, because he'd loved Anna and he never thought he'd feel that way about any woman again.

Which was why he put distance between them. Katie would never be his.

He glanced outside and saw the sky had turned dark. He had filled his cart with nonperishables. He grabbed a few snacks before he headed to the register area to pay.

Rachel's husband, Jed, grinned as Micah approached. He was manning the cash register in front while Rachel was in the back where she made sandwiches and other food items.

"Did you find everything you need?" Jed asked with a smile.

"I hope so." Micah glanced out the window. "Looks like a storm is on its way."

"*Ja*, I hope it's a quick one."

"Me, too. I'm worried about our farm animals outside." He needed to get home to ensure their safety, but it would be difficult with the children.

His concern must have been apparent, because with a thoughtful, smiling look at Eliza and Jacob,

Jed offered, "Why don't you head home to check on them? We can keep the children here until you get back. No need to hurry. With this storm, the store wouldn't be busy for a while."

"I don't want to impose." Micah had come to know the King family well since moving to New Berne. It wasn't that he didn't trust them with his son and daughters because he did. He wished that Katie was here. His children were afraid of thunderstorms, and Katie would soothe them and make them feel safe.

Rachel approached from the back of the store, holding Rebecca. "What's wrong?" she said as if feeling Micah's concern, just as thunder rumbled in the distance.

"Storm," Jed told her. "Micah needs to get to the farm to get his livestock inside. I suggested it's better if he leaves the children here with us, but he worries that he'll be imposing."

The woman laughed. "Micah, I assure you that I will enjoy every moment with your little ones. Mine are with my in-laws. Now that they are getting older, I miss having young children."

"Micah, leave them here. Please! I like to see my wife happy." Jed grabbed Jacob's hat from the shopping cart and settled it on his little head. He grinned when Jacob took off his hat and put it carefully back inside the cart. "To tell you the truth, I enjoy little ones as much as Rachel does. And we promise not to get them all sugared up so they're a handful when you come for them."

Micah widened his eyes at the thought of having rambunctious children due to sweets. "I'd appreciate it." He lowered his voice so that they wouldn't hear. "They're afraid of thunderstorms." He turned toward his son and bent down to explain the situation with Jacob. "You'll stay with Rachel and Jed. I have to take care of your *grossdaddi*'s livestock."

Jacob met the other man's gaze, and Jed smiled at him in reassurance. "We'll fix you a *gut* lunch," he said. "And if your *vadder* says it's fine, we'll have cake or cookies afterward." His gaze met Micah's. "Just enough for a boy of Jacob's size," he said.

Micah nodded. "They usually go in for a nap by now, but I don't know if they will sleep as long as they can hear the storm. They've been amazingly *gut* all morning, but I can't guarantee they will stay that way."

"We have a storage room in the back that is quiet and private. We can put them down to nap on some quilts that we store there."

"But don't you usually sell them?"

"Nay," Rachel said. "These belong to our family."

"They were for our children when we had to work late," Jed explained. "Now they're too old for naps."

Micah said goodbye to his little ones and then a few minutes later, he was on his way back to his parents' farm, convinced that the children would be fine with Jed and Rachel. The storm picked up in intensity as he steered the buggy along the road. He kept on the blacktop, afraid that if he went too far off the side that his vehicle would get stuck in a water-filled ditch or, worse, tip over.

The downpour was nearly blinding as he parked the buggy close to the barn on his family's property.

He hurriedly got out and raced to check the pasture where the animals were situated. To his immense relief, he saw that the cows and goats had congregated under a lean-to within the fence. They would be fine there.

Rain dripped off his hat and soaked his clothes. Micah ran back to the barn where he untied his horse, opened the door and led the animal inside. Thunder crashed overhead. Lightning flashed through the loft window. He headed toward the front stall where he usually kept his mare Jenny and was surprised to find it already occupied, with a strange horse's head peeking at him over the stable door. With a frown, he looked back outside and saw a pony cart, which, in his haste to check on the animals, he hadn't noticed until now. After closing the barn door, he looked in the stall door currently housing the unfamiliar horse, and that was when he saw her huddled in one corner, eyes closed, shivering, her hair and clothes wet. *Katie Mast.* His breath caught when he realized that she was here. He moved his horse down the main barn corridor and tied him to a support post.

When he returned to Katie, she stirred and gasped with alarm as he opened the stall door.

"Katie, it's me—Micah," he said as he entered the stall. He reached down to help her stand.

"I'm so sorry, Micah!" Her blue eyes were filled with remorse. "I was driving home when it started to rain. I didn't want to bother you…so I took shelter here."

"Katie, it's fine. I wouldn't want you out in this storm. It's getting much worse." As if to prove him right, lightning lit up the barn interior, followed by a deafening huge thunder boom.

Micah saw Katie jump and fought the strongest urge to pull her into his arms. He watched her wrap her arms around herself, and he left the stall to find a blanket.

"Where are you going?" she asked, clearly nervous about the storm.

He softened his gaze. "Not far. You're wet and cold." He saw her swallow hard. "Come here," he said as he grabbed a bale of straw. "Have a seat." He helped her to sit. "I'll be right back." He started to leave.

"Micah!" she called. He faced her. "Where are the children?"

He smiled. "Safe. They're with Rachel and Jed King at the store."

She nodded, looking relieved until a crack of thunder frightened her, and she hugged herself with her arms.

When he returned quickly, as promised, Micah felt her relax. He'd retrieved a large quilt and a flashlight from a shelf along one wall of the barn.

"Found this," he said, unfolding it. He turned on the flashlight and set it down, then he wrapped her up in the quilt. "This should keep you warm."

"Micah, I'm soaked."

"*Ja*, which is why you need this." He worked to make sure she was fully covered. "Hold on to the ends to keep it closed."

Katie obeyed. "What about you? You're just as wet."

"I'm fine." He picked up the flashlight and sat

on the barn floor beside her. She was beautiful. She looked vulnerable with her wet hair and her prayer *kapp* slightly askew. He could see her glistening blue eyes in the lamplight. Softening, Micah fought the strongest urge to remove her head covering so that she would be more comfortable. "Are you *oll recht*?"

She nodded. Katie felt safe whenever Micah was nearby. What was she doing? She shouldn't be feeling this way about him. Jacob had been the one meant to be her husband and when he died… Shivering, she stared at the ground and away from the one man she couldn't seem to forget.

Micah began to engage her in conversation. "I warned Rachel that my *kinner* usually nap at this time…"

"They will be fine," she said with a soft smile. "Rachel can handle them. She is an experienced mother with children of her own." Because of Micah, Katie was starting to relax despite the intensity of the storm raging outside. Fortunately, the barn roof was solid without a single leak.

"Tell me about your family." Micah shifted closer as if trying to gain warmth from her quilt-wrapped body. Katie was tempted to open the quilt and offer him space but she didn't. Because she knew it would be wrong.

"What do you want to know?"

"I understand you have three *bruders* and two *schweschters*. Who is the oldest? Uri?"

She shook her head, amused. "I am."

"*Nay*, impossible," he said, and she frowned at

him. He arched an eyebrow. "You are too pretty and young to be the oldest child in the Mervin Mast family."

"Micah…" She loved what he'd said, but this situation, their proximity with the storm outside creating a cozy and odd sense of intimacy, an intimacy that made her feel things she had no right to feel, made her breath catch as every one of her senses grew active and aware. She gazed at him, comparing his features to her deceased betrothed, but the only face she could see now was Micah's. Somehow, she'd lost the memory of Jacob. Which made her feel more than a little guilty. And sad.

Upset with herself, she looked away.

"Katie, what's wrong?"

She shook her head, unwilling to confess the truth.

"Tell me," he urged with a look of concern.

Katie briefly held his gaze before she looked down, anywhere but at him. He was so handsome that he stole her breath every time she saw him. The ease of their conversation had only brought home to her how much she wished things were different, that he wasn't a widower who only wanted a mother for his children. That he was seeking a wife he could love.

"I'm fine, Micah." Warmer now, Katie unwrapped the quilt and offered it to him.

His blue gaze seemed to regard her thoughtfully "I don't need it, but *danki*."

She nodded and stood. She felt anxious suddenly, and she wished that the storm would pass so that she could be on her way home—and away from Micah. Not that she wanted to leave him, but considering the way she was feeling right now, she thought it would be best if she could put distance between them.

Following her lead, Micah rose. "The storm doesn't look like it will be ending soon," he said after they'd heard another reverberating rumble of thunder.

The horses inside the barn shifted slightly but didn't seem overly bothered.

Katie wished that *Gott* had chosen a different path for her. One that didn't include a dead fiancé and an older brother who had loved his wife too much to fall in love again.

She faced him, studying him, wanting to preserve these last moments to take out as memories later when Micah married and her remembrances would be all that she had left of their time together.

A sharp, loud crack from above startled her, making her cry out. Micah reached for her, pulling her close, as the scent of smoke assaulted her nose. She glanced up to see bright flames along the barn ceiling, smelled the burning wood.

"Micah!" she cried. "Look! The barn is on fire!"

Micah released her and focused his gaze on the ceiling, where a small fire from a lightning strike grew quickly along the barn roof, fed by the wind.

"Katie!" He caught her by the shoulders, turning her to fully face him. "We need to free the animals," he said calmly. "Help me open the back door so we can release them into the pasture."

Micah's unruffled demeanor gave Katie a sense of purpose and worked to settle her fears of the storm.

She couldn't allow innocent livestock to be injured or killed. She raced to help Micah with the rear barn door, then she pushed and prodded each horse until they were out of the burning building and into the field. Micah ran ahead and opened a gate that led to another pasture far from the flames. With a wild cry, he herded the horses through the open gate then returned to the barn.

Smoke filled the interior of the structure until Katie could barely see. There was one horse left, and she hurried to set it free. Micah appeared at her side. "That's Joe. My *dat*'s gelding," he said as he took the reins from her to help the animal outside. "He's injured. I'll bring him out. Katie, we've done what we could. Please get out of the barn now."

"Just let me take one last look to see if we missed any," she cried. Unable to leave until she knew for certain that every animal was safe, Katie ignored his concern and ran through the smoke to search for livestock she might have missed. She coughed as she found a mother and baby goats still inside. She urged them outside, then took one last look and realized that every animal that was inside had been evacuated.

"Micah," she cried. "Our vehicles! They're too close to the barn!"

Together, Micah and Katie worked to alternately push and pull three vehicles away from the burning structure.

Moments later, from a safe distance, Katie stood in the pouring rain with Micah, watching with horror as the Bontragers' barn crumbled on itself, destroyed by fire. The pouring rain did little to nothing to fight the flames and heat. "I'm going next door to call the fire department!" she cried, suddenly spurred into action.

"Katie!" Micah called out. "Be careful!"

She nodded. She then raced across the street and banged on the neighboring Englisher's door. A young male answered and stared at her, his eyes widening as he looked at her with mounting horror. "Are you all right?" he asked.

"*Ja.* I'm fine. We got the animals out. I'd hoped to use your phone."

"I already called the fire department," he told her. "They're on their way."

"Danki!" she cried before she raced back across the street, grateful that there were no oncoming vehicles to stop her from hurrying to Micah.

Micah stared with dismay at the flame-ridden outbuilding as Katie reached his side. "Micah," she murmured, briefly running a hand along his arm soothingly.

He didn't immediately acknowledge her presence. His masculine face was layered with soot, and she realized that she, too, must be covered.

The rain slowed to a drizzle as the storm started to move on. Black rivulets, resembling dark tears, cascaded down Micah's face. His hat was gone, no doubt left and destroyed in the barn, and black dust clung to his brown hair, along his neck and over his clothes to his muddy boots. He seemed lost, and Katie wanted to comfort him.

"Micah," she said softly.

Without meeting her gaze, he reached out and clasped her hand, interlocking their fingers. He stood quietly for a moment, keeping her close. She gave his fingers a gentle squeeze to show that she was here for him.

"*Danki*, Katie," he said, his voice raspy.

Sirens screamed in the distance and strengthened as the fire trucks drew near. Two vehicles pulled onto the property with flashing red lights. Ten firefighters climbed out of the vehicles. A water truck drove in and parked next to the other trucks. Two firemen unrolled the hose away from the water truck, and three others helped the hose along while two firefighters raced toward the burning barn, one with the hose nozzle in his hand.

"Miss. Sir," an older fireman said from behind them, "please step out of this immediate area so we can do our job."

Micah nodded and, still clasping Katie's hand, drew her away from the barn and toward the house. Fortunately, the downpour had wet the main residence enough to keep it safe from sparks that could set the house on fire. Micah continued to pull her with him to the front of the house and closer to the street, a safe distance from the men from the fire department. Katie watched helplessly as the firefighters fought to put out the raging fire. The fire was put out, but it was too late to save the old barn.

Katie didn't care if she was wet and sooty. Micah held her hand, and she was glad she could be there for him; he needed someone. Needed her.

Having heard the sirens while some had caught

sight of the flames, the Bontragers' neighbors and fellow church members arrived within the hour with offers of assistance. The fire had been put out, but smoke from the smoldering embers hung heavily in the damp air. Gabriel Fisher approached, and Micah quickly released her hand. Katie felt the loss of his grip as he left her to greet him and the others who had come to help.

"Micah, I can take your goats to shelter," Gabriel Fisher said. He'd been burned in a house fire years ago, and Katie knew that Gabriel had firsthand experience with the devastation caused by fire. "We don't have a large farm like you do, but we certainly have room in an outbuilding on our property." He smiled. "Lucy wants to get goats, but I suggested she wait until after she gives birth to make a decision. This will give her an opportunity to feed and care for them."

Katie, standing next to Micah, smiled at him. "A wise suggestion," she agreed.

"*Danki*, Gabriel," Micah said. "My family will appreciate this."

Levi Yost stepped up to him next. He had come with Gabriel, which shouldn't have surprised Katie, but it did, since Levi's wife was Lucy's deceased first husband Harley Schwartz's sister. "We'll take your cows," the man offered pleasantly. "I've got me plenty of room for the whole lot of them until after the barn raising."

Aaron Hostetler, an experienced construction worker, approached next. "I'll order the material for the new barn. I'm thinking we can have everything here in a week or so."

"*Danki*, Aaron," Micah said, his voice gravelly from the smoke.

Katie could tell that Micah was deeply moved by the concern and offers of assistance. She knew the animals could probably stay temporarily in the lean-tos on Evan's property, but then Micah would have to worry about caring for them alone until his family returned—and with three children to tend to, it would be difficult.

She joined a group of women who had congregated in a gathering away from their men. She heard Mary King speak as she approached.

"We need to figure out the food for the barn raising," Mary said. "Kings will donate several large containers of salad and a platter of roast beef."

"I'll bring vegetables and some ham," Nancy Yost, Lucy Fisher's former sister-in-law, said. "I'm sure Lucy will want to contribute. I'll do what I can to help her since she tires more easily these days."

"I'll make desserts," Katie said with a smile. "I love to bake, and Mam and I will also bring sweet and sour green beans."

She glanced toward Micah and wished she could go up to him and give him a hug. She could tell he was overwhelmed by what had happened. He looked lost as he stood among the men who were deep in discussion about their plans to hold a barn raising for the Bontrager family as soon as the material was on-site. After excusing herself, Katie left the women and headed in Micah's direction. The men dispersed, passing by her as they joined their wives then proceeded to their vehicles.

"Micah?" she said softly, alarmed by the look of devastation in his blue eyes. "Micah, everything will be *oll recht*."

He turned toward her with a pained expression. "Will it?"

She blinked, stunned by the change in him. "It will. How can I help?" She knew he was a kind man, but the disastrous fire and its damage, while his family was away, was apparently way more than he could handle.

"What am I going to tell my *vadder* and *mudder*?" he asked, his jaw tight, his blue eyes filled with concern.

"Have you spoken with them recently?"

"The other day. They decided to stay with my *grosseldra* another few days." He sighed. "What can I say to them?"

"The truth, Micah. You tell them what happened. That a storm caused a barn fire and their animals were saved—and no one was hurt."

His expression softened as he gazed at her. "*Danki*, Katie."

"Your *kinner*?" Katie basked under the comforting glow of his blue gaze. "I'm sure they are waiting for you to bring them home."

A car pulled into the driveway, and a man stepped out. Katie recognized Bert Hadden, an Englisher who frequently gave rides to members of her Amish community. "I thought I might be able to help."

Katie stepped up to him. "You can. Will you give

Micah and me a ride after we get cleaned up a little? His children are at Kings General Store." Hoping that her presence offered comfort, she decided that she would stay with Micah while he picked up his children. She wondered, though, if it wouldn't be better for Micah if Jacob and the girls spent the night with the Kings. But that was up to Micah and the Kings. She and Micah were both too tired to round up their horses and hitch them to their vehicles. That task would be held for tomorrow.

Chapter Eleven

It was midmorning the day after the fire, and his children were still asleep. Worried about his family's reaction to the loss of their barn, Micah had lain awake all night. He was so tired, but there was too much to do to think about resting. He studied the charred structure from inside the house, through the screened door. The sounds of bird song filtered in, reminding him that life continued as it always did. The scent of smoke hung heavily in the air, reminding him of the horror of the fire. Still, he was grateful that no one was hurt. Katie was fine, and he was fine. *Thanks be to Gott.*

The site needed to be cleared before the new structure was built. He hadn't been able to get a hold of his parents to tell them the bad news. Micah didn't want to worry them or have them come home early. His grandparents needed them, and he could take care of things here. A barn raising was scheduled, and he wanted to assure them that everything would be fine. But for them not to know? It didn't feel right, which was why yesterday afternoon, while in Kings General Store, he'd called and left a message at Smith's Market, the business closest to his grandparents' Indiana home.

Yesterday, after Bert had driven him with Katie to pick up his children, Micah had walked inside the store, after taking the time to clean up and change clothes, and he tried not to show his concern about what had happened. Having Katie with him had helped greatly. She too had cleaned up at his parents' house, and Micah had found a spare dress that belonged to his sister Emma.

Something about Katie soothed and settled him. He'd been grateful for her company as they rode to Kings, even more so as they entered the building. Jacob and his girls had been happy to see him, but when his little ones saw Katie, they'd cried out with joy and reached for her. Amazing, he thought as the memory hit him of Katie holding his daughters, one in each arm.

Rachel and Jed had offered to keep his children overnight, but Micah had wanted them home with him. As Bert drove them home after dropping off Katie, he feared his children's reactions to the ruined barn.

Dat! Jacob had cried, his eyes wide, when he saw the charred remains in the car's headlights after they had climbed out of the vehicle.

The roof caught on fire, he explained.

But how?

It happened during the storm, but don't worry.

Our neighbors are holding a barn raising for us, and there will be a new barn in its place soon.

Where are all of grossdaddi*'s animals?*

They're safe, soohn, he assured him. *Our friends and neighbors took them until the new barn is ready.*

Thankfully, his explanation had satisfied his son, a fact that surprised Micah whenever he thought about it. He expected Jacob to be upset more over the fire, but then who knew what was in the mind of a nearly four-year-old? His worry eased. *The resilience of young, innocent children.* After supper, his little ones had crashed and gone to bed early, leaving Micah concerned about speaking with his father.

He smiled as he thought of Katie. They had both looked a mess after the fire with their hair and faces blackened and their clothes covered with soot, which was why he'd offered her his sister's dress. She'd been reluctant at first, but then she finally agreed.

The soft rumble of a car engine from the road, getting louder by the second, drew him back to the present. Micah opened the door and stepped outside just as a white van pulled close to the house and parked. When he saw his parents and his siblings climb down from the vehicle, he felt his stomach turn. He stepped out onto the porch and watched his family gaze at the ruins left by the fire.

"Dat. Mam," Micah said, drawing their attention as he approached them.

His father turned first, and Micah was shocked that his parent was surprisingly calm. Dat met him halfway. "What happened, *soohn*?"

"Lightning strike during yesterday's thunderstorm." Micah ran a hand across the back of his neck. "Katie and I were in the barn when it hit. We were able to get the livestock out safely. Our neighbors are housing them until the new barn is built."

Evan shook his head. "You and Katie were in the barn? Are you *oll recht*? Is Katie?"

Micah nodded. "*Ja*, we're fine. We were able to save the animals before the roof collapsed." He saw his mother approach. "The barn raising will be quick, thanks to your neighbors and friends. Jed King said that we can make it happen by a week from Tuesday—and possibly sooner." It was Saturday, and the charred wood and debris had to be taken away before they prepared the site for the new structure. "I'll work on clearing the ground. Dat, you, Mam and everyone can head inside to rest. You must be weary after your trip." He was too but he'd never admit it.

"Mam," he greeted as his mother joined him and Dat. He felt terrible that his parents had come home to the mess. "I called Smith's and left a message yesterday for you to call. I had no idea that you were already on your way home."

"We left yesterday morning. My *vadder* is doing well enough to travel," his mother said. "We decided that Mam and Dat should move to New Berne, and your *grosseldra* agreed. Your *vadder* wants to build a *dawdi haus* for them here on the farm." She glanced toward the barn. "But seeing this now… I don't know…"

"We'll get their *haus* built, Mam," Micah assured them. "*Grossdaddi and grossmudder* need to live close to us. The new barn won't take long with our church community's help. Jonathan, Vern and Matt will build their *dawdi haus* with me."

"But what of your own *haus*, Micah?" his *vadder* asked. His face was drawn from the ordeal of the trip and his father-in-law's illness. For the first time, Micah thought his *dat* looked much older than his forty-eight years.

"I'm not worried about my *haus*, Dat. It's nearly done. I've been working on the floors in the bedrooms. The downstairs is move-in ready." Micah ran a hand raggedly through his hair. "I'm sorry you had to come home to this."

"Soohn," his father said. *"Gott* gives us only what we can handle. You saved our animals and everyone is *oll recht*. What more can we ask for?" He frowned. "Where are my *kinskinner*?"

"In their rooms, sleeping. They stayed with Rachel and Jed King during the storm yesterday while I came back to check on the animals. They didn't nap for long and were tired when they came home. I need to check on them."

"May I?" Mam said.

Micah smiled at his mother. *"Ja,* of course, Mam. They're your *kinskinner*. They'll be excited to see you."

His sister Addie joined him and their father. "Micah…"

"Lightning," his *dat* said before Micah had a chance to explain.

"Ach nay!" Addie said. "That must have been terrible for you! When did it happen?"

"Yesterday," Micah said. "Katie and I were able to save our livestock. Except for the horses, Gabriel

Fisher and Levi Yost are sheltering the animals until we replace the barn." He frowned. "Where's Emma?"

"She and Matthew stayed behind to help your *grosseldra*," Dat said.

Addie studied the barn with a frown. "That was kind of our neighbors to help." She paused. "So, Katie was here?"

"*Ja.* She was on her way home from Lucy Fisher's when the storm hit. When I came home to check on the animals, I discovered Katie had sought shelter in our barn. No sooner had I brought Jenny in out of the bad weather when lightning set fire to the roof." He smiled as he thought of the amazing young woman who had sprung into action to assist him. "Without Katie's help, we would have lost a lot of them."

"Thank the Lord that you came home and she was there to help," Dat said.

"*Ja,*" Micah agreed. *Ja. Thank Gott for Katie Mast.*

Katie held a casserole on her lap as she rode with her family to the Bontrager farm. After they'd heard about the barn fire, her parents and siblings wanted to see what they could do to help.

"*Ach nay!*" her mother exclaimed when she saw the black remains of the barn.

"*Ja*, it was bad."

"We can clear away the charred debris," Uri suggested as he leaned forward as their father pulled their vehicle onto the property.

A van passed by them on its way back to the road. Katie saw Evan with some of his children staring at the barn. As her father drove closer to the house, Micah turned, his gaze immediately catching hold of hers through the buggy's open side window.

"I'm sorry to see this, Evan," Dat said sincerely when he joined his friend in the yard. "Gabriel Fisher let us know what happened before Katie got home. There is much to be done before the material for the new barn is delivered next week." Her father raised his straw hat and settled it back onto his head. "Best to get it cleaned up before one of the children wanders over and gets hurt."

Katie agreed. She stared at the ruined barn and recalled how frightened she'd been when she'd seen the fire caused by lightning. Yet, when it came time, she'd jumped to help Micah, no longer afraid of anything in her quest to save livestock. Micah had that effect on her.

The sound of wagon wheels had them turning as vehicles belonging to their fellow church members came onto the property. Katie saw the Hostetler brothers drive in followed by Gabriel and Lucy Fisher with their children. David Bontrager, the preacher, had brought his neighbors, the Yoders. The young male Englisher who had called the fire department crossed the street after seeing all the activity, wanting to help.

Men stepped out of their buggies with their sons. Two wives, who accompanied their husbands, brought food like Katie and her mother.

Rachel King wore a grim look as she stared at the barn before she approached Katie who still stood in the yard. "Katie," she breathed, "I had no idea.

When I think of what could have happened to you and Micah… Weren't you afraid?"

Katie nodded. "*Ja*, terrified, but then Micah remained calm as he and I ran to save the animals, and I was too busy to be afraid. In fact, Micah told me to leave at one point, but I just couldn't—not until I knew for certain that every one of them was out of danger."

"Thank the Lord that you're *oll recht*."

Ja, praise the Lord, Katie thought as Rachel left to put food in the house. She shuddered when she thought about how things could have turned out differently. If something had happened to Micah… She offered up a prayer of thanks that Micah and she were fine.

It was ten in the morning, and the yard filled with activity as the men moved around the burnt wreckage, discussing the best way to clear the site before they dove into the job. Katie watched, pleased, as her brothers quickly went to work, followed by Micah and his brothers—and both of their fathers.

"You two start on the back side of the building," Uri directed to Joseph and Abraham, easily taking charge. "*Bruders*, be careful. I'd doubt there still are hot embers, but it doesn't hurt to be cautious. Just hover your hand over the area you want to work on. If you don't feel any heat, go for it!"

"Uri, where should we pile everything?" Joseph asked.

The oldest of her younger brothers looked around. "Let's stack it over there."

Katie watched as they moved the garbage to a

cleared area away to the far left of the barn. *A good choice.*

The volunteers' faces, hands and clothing became filthy with soot as they toiled to get the job done. It was well past noon when the women convinced them to break for a meal.

"You need sustenance to finish," Betty said.

Katie watched the workers wash up at the water pump before they headed to the food table outside, where they grabbed and loaded up their plates. Her attention was drawn to Micah, who was covered in soot, his head bare, as he ate. As if sensing her regard, he turned and locked gazes with her. She gave him a little smile and nod, but to her dismay, he watched her without expression a few seconds before he threw out his paper plate and went back to work.

An engine roared as a massive dump truck pulled onto the dirt driveway and entered the yard. Bert Hadden, the English friend of their community, parked the truck and got out. "Load 'er up," he said.

Soon, the garbage was gone and the site of the old barn clear of all rubble.

Katie helped pack up leftover food and clean dishes. When the work was done, she, her mother and sisters went out to the buggy to wait for her father and brothers to join them.

Betty approached them. "*Danki*, Katie," she said. "You have truly been a blessing."

At a loss, Katie could only gape at her. "Betty, I haven't done anything."

"That's not what Micah said."

Katie felt a rush of pleasure as she wondered what Micah had told her.

Her mother placed a hand on her shoulder. "She has always been a *gut dochter*. I don't know what I would have done without her all these years."

Katie looked at her with surprise. "Mam…"

"It's true, *dochter*. When I was sick right after Abraham was born, you took care of your siblings, including Abraham, and you were just a child."

She blushed. "I… I should see what's taking Dat and my *bruders so long*." Katie was eager to escape. She didn't like being the center of attention. She hadn't done anything any daughter or friend wouldn't have done for someone who needed them.

Escaping the females, Katie approached the men conversing in a group near the barn site. She heard them talking as she drew closer to them.

"We'll come back early Monday to finish up," she heard her father say.

"Not necessary," Micah said, his voice pleasant. "My *bruders* and I can handle it."

Dat looked as if he wanted to argue, but it was Evan's barn and land, and if this was what his friend wanted, she knew her father would respect his wishes.

"*Ja*, we'll be fine, Merv," Evan said. "We appreciate your help today."

Her father nodded. "Who's ordering the lumber?"

"Jed King and Aaron Hostetler." Micah ran a hand along the back of his neck, unknowingly spreading black across his nape.

"That's *gut*," Dat said. "Both have construction experience."

Their faces and clothes were black with soot. Mud caked their shoes, and Katie saw patches of it on their elbows and knees where they must have knelt while working.

Katie stepped back to wait patiently for her father's attention.

Micah saw her outside the fringe of the men's gathering. "Katie."

She blushed. She didn't want them to think she was eavesdropping.

Her father turned to her with a frown. *"Dochter..."*

She pulled her gaze from Micah to meet her father's. "I didn't mean to interrupt you. We weren't sure if you were ready to leave." She turned to go. "You're busy. I'll tell Mam and we'll wait inside with Betty."

"Nay," he replied, drawing her attention. "I'm ready." Dat addressed his friends. "I'll see you at service tomorrow."

Evan smiled at him. *"Danki,* Merv."

"No need to thank me," her father replied. "You'd do the same for me if our positions were reversed."

"Ja, I would," his friend agreed.

Katie started to turn when she felt Micah's intense gaze on her. She started across the yard. She wasn't there to listen in. Did Micah think she was?

"Wait up, Katie," her father called. She watched him signal to her brothers to follow before he hurriedly reached her side.

She shifted uncomfortably, expecting a reprimand from him. "I wasn't eavesdropping, Dat."

Her father looked at her with surprise. "I didn't

think you were." His warm smile eased the nervous butterflies in her stomach. "You did a *gut* thing yesterday when you helped Micah. It scares me to think about what might have happened to the both of you. I believe *Gott* was watching over you, so I will think only of the positive and not what could have been."

"Dat, I shuddered to think about what could have happened," she told him as she reached the area where her mother and sisters waited. Her brothers walked past and arrived at the buggy before the two of them.

"But it didn't." Her father eyed her thoughtfully. "You did a fine thing, Katie."

"I just did what anyone would do."

Dat smiled. "I don't think that's true, *dochter*. I doubt another woman would have stayed in a burning barn to help. It was a noble thing you did, and Micah had nothing but *gut* things to say about your role in saving their animals. Now let's go home." He waved her to go ahead of him and Katie obeyed, climbing inside the vehicle to sit beside her sisters.

As her father drove their buggy toward home, Katie marveled that Micah had mentioned her at all. He hadn't seemed happy to see her this morning. In fact, every time their gazes collided, he looked away. He seemed distant…his expression stoic…as if she wasn't worth his time.

It had been three days since he'd told her he wouldn't be needing her to babysit. And now that Betty and Evan were home, Katie knew that her time with his little ones was most definitely over. She stared out the window at the passing scenery. Would

Micah ask her to watch the children once he moved them into his newly renovated house? Or would she no longer be needed—or wanted?

Katie felt an ache in her chest, a pain that reminded her that she had begun to regard Micah as more than a friend. Her throat tightened and she had difficulty swallowing,

Micah needs a wife, and I... I can't marry, she reminded herself. She couldn't take the chance of losing someone she loved again.

Loved? Nay, she didn't love Micah. *I can't possibly love him.* Katie closed her eyes, upset with the painful direction of her thoughts. It would be best for Micah—and her, she assured herself—if Naomi found him a wife soon.

It would be best for all of them. She sighed. And she would learn to get by with her sewing business and the memory of Jacob, the man she'd loved and lost.

Chapter Twelve

Everyone attended Sunday service at the Jed King residence. Katie knew the second Micah and his family arrived that morning for church. She felt the air change and thicken inside the house at the exact moment she saw Micah enter with his family. She couldn't seem to take her gaze off him. Micah looked extremely handsome in his white shirt, black vest and black pants. He had taken off his wide-brimmed black felt hat, his Sunday best, and his light brown hair looked clean and soft. His blue eyes were bright in a face that was masculine and riveting. She saw him smile at the preacher's wife, his teeth a flash of white above his beard. Katie willed him to look in her direction, but he didn't. He made his way through the Kings' great room and took a seat with his father and brothers.

The space was filled with men and their older sons in one section and women with young children in another. When his gaze swept over the women's section, he didn't pause to acknowledge her. It was almost as if he was distancing himself from her again. She drew a painful breath. The time they'd spent together working side by side to evacuate the animals during the fire might never have happened.

Betty and her daughter Addie sat directly in front of Katie and her mother. Addie held little Jacob on her lap while Betty was attempting to hold both of her squirming granddaughters. Seeing Betty struggle, Katie tapped her on the shoulder. "May I help?" she asked with a smile for the girls.

"I'd appreciate it," Betty said with a grin before she allowed Katie to pull Micah's youngest into her arms.

"That was a nice thing to do, *dochter*," her mother whispered as the little girl snuggled against Katie.

She smiled at her *mam* who eyed her with approval. "Betty needed help."

The service began with a hymn and everyone stood. Katie held Eliza on her hip and sang along with the congregation. As she sat down again, she sensed someone staring at her. She was surprised to see it was Micah. His gaze dropped for a moment to his daughter in her arms, and she noted a softening of his expression…until his face became unreadable as his attention returned to Katie.

Hurt, she averted her eyes. She thought they'd become friends but she was wrong. Sick to her stomach, she had trouble concentrating on the preacher's sermon. She tried to focus on what the man was saying, but her mind kept drifting to Jacob, her deceased betrothed…and Micah, his older brother, who was very much alive.

Three hours after it started, the service ended, and Katie was relieved. She wanted to go home to avoid any interaction with Micah. She loved the Bontragers. They were like a second family to her, but Micah apparently didn't much care for her. She had no idea why. They had gotten along fine when she first watched his children. Until three days later when the man told her he wouldn't have use of her babysitting services the following day because he was taking a break from his house renovations and would be home with his children. It had been five days since he'd told her not to come. Apparently, he no longer needed her.

Katie helped in the kitchen with food and even managed to smile when she saw the fresh homemade bread and peanut butter provided by Rachel and Jed. Peanut butter on fresh bread was a traditional meal to share with the church community after service, although members of her congregation enjoyed adding other dishes to the meal, especially desserts. Theirs was a small district. Katie and her family used to belong to a much larger church district of about 59 families north of New Berne. It had taken over an hour to get to service, and traveling time meant leaving home early and getting back late. Then Bishop Amos Miller in his wisdom had decided that it would be better to start another district right in New Berne.

Two long tables were placed up along one wall in Jed and Rachel's great room for food, and the men had set up folding tables for eating. Katie carried dishes to the food table until she finally found her mother in the kitchen alone.

"Mam, I'd like to ask Uri to take me home."

Her mother's expression immediately filled with concern. "What's wrong?"

"I feel sick. I thought I'd lie down for a while this afternoon."

"Would it help to eat?"

"Nay," she whispered, upset. "I can't eat anything right now." She placed a hand over her churning stomach.

Mam's face softened. *"Ja,* of course, you may go home. It won't take long for your *bruder* to eat. Ask him when he's finished."

The burning sensation in her belly had gotten worse. She knew it had something to do with Micah's stoic expression and lack of smile whenever their gazes met.

Despite feeling unwell, Katie served food to the men and then stepped away to wait until her brother finished his meal. She'd avoided Micah. His distance since telling her that he no longer needed her to watch his children hurt and she felt…unwanted.

Uri finished eating and stood, chatting with a group of young men, including their brothers, Abraham and Joseph, and Lucy Fisher's brother Seth. Katie approached him before he became involved with a baseball game with his friends. The others had stepped away and only Seth remained with her brother.

"Uri," she called. *"Bruder,* may I talk with you for a second?"

"Ja, Katie," he replied with a frown. "Seth, I'll see you outside."

Seth nodded. In her estimate, Seth Graber was a

wonderful young man, and Katie knew that his sister Lucy felt the same way.

"What do you need?" Uri asked her, eyeing her with curiosity.

She sighed, closed her eyes briefly. "Would you please take me home? I'm not feeling well."

"*Ja*, of course, I will. Is there anything else I can do? Does Mam know?"

"She does." Katie glanced toward the window to see a group of young men assemble out in the yard. "Baseball?" She placed a hand over her churning stomach.

"*Ja*, but it's not important. I can take you home then come back, if you'll be all right by yourself at the *haus*." He studied her with concern.

"I'll be fine. I just want to lie down for a while."

Uri continued to eye her with worry. "Katie…"

"*Danki, bruder.* I just want this afternoon to rest and recover. I'm sure I'll be fine tomorrow."

"I'll meet you at our buggy," he said.

Katie nodded. "I'll let Mam know you're taking me home." She watched Uri walk away and was aware that he was concerned, but she couldn't confide in him—or anyone—about why she was feeling ill. She shouldn't feel this way. She would be fine. She'd loved Jacob with everything inside her. Now, after realizing she felt similar—but more powerful— feelings for Micah she felt terribly guilty. How could she forget Jacob so quickly?

"I'm sorry, Jacob," she whispered. "You're all that I ever wanted, but… I didn't mean to fall for him. I'm so, so sorry."

Katie told her mother where she was going and

headed to meet Uri in the family buggy. As she walked up to the vehicle, a man stepped out in front of her. Micah.

"I'm sorry you don't feel well, Katie," Micah said. "I told Uri that I'll take you home."

She shook her head. "You don't have to do that."

"I want to," he said. "I'd like to talk with you." Micah held her gaze until she had to look away.

"Fine." Uncomfortable with the situation, she couldn't do anything about it without calling attention to the problem between them. She didn't want her—or his—family to know.

Micah could feel the tension coming off Katie in waves. Uri had told him that she wasn't well. Concerned, he'd offered to be the one to take her home, and Katie's brother had agreed. As they reached his wagon, he held out a hand to help her climb up. He noted her hesitation before she accepted his assistance. Her small hand felt warm and fragile within his grasp. He heard her gasp when he lifted her up onto the wooden seat.

Katie didn't look at him but stared straight ahead as he climbed up into the wagon to sit next to her. He grabbed hold of the leathers. "You haven't eaten," he said softly.

She shot him a quick look. "I'm not hungry."

He nodded, and then with a flick of the reins, he eased forward out from the row of parked vehicles and steered his wagon toward the road.

Katie didn't say a word to him as he drove onto the street and toward the Mervin Mast property. He needed to clear the air between them. Micah knew that he hadn't sought her out for a conversation since the fire. Soon the lumber for the new barn would arrive, and he had so much to think about and do. He'd learned this morning that the lumber would arrive this Tuesday, not the following Tuesday as anticipated.

"Katie," he murmured, finally drawing her attention. "Can I get you something that will help you feel better?"

She shook her head. "*Nay*, I just need to lie down for a while. I'll be fine."

"I hope it helps." He gave her a soft smile.

She blinked as if taken aback.

"What?" he asked.

"You…" She sighed and looked away.

"I what?"

"You told me you didn't need me to babysit because your family would be home soon. But then they stayed longer and you didn't ask me to come back."

"I know." He felt awful for making her feel unwanted. His feelings were more than he should have for her, which was why he'd made the decision to keep his distance. Something he was afraid he was no longer able to do. Like today he'd been unable to stay away from her.

Silence reigned as he drove closer to her father's farm. He steered his horse onto the Mast property, upset that he didn't know what to say to ease the tension between them. He parked close to the house. Katie turned to climb down.

He touched her arm to stop her. "Katie." She stiffened but met his gaze. "I'm sorry. I've had a lot to deal with, and I didn't mean to keep you from watching and spending time with my *kinner*. It's clear that they love you." Although he wasn't sure that was a good thing. "Once we move into the new house, I'd like you to watch them again." He felt her relax a little, and her eyes held on to his.

"Micah, if you don't want me to babysit for you, all you have to do is say so. *Oke?*"

He nodded and thought how pretty she looked in her Sunday best dress of royal blue. The cape and apron over her dress were white while her head covering was black, a color that unmarried women frequently wore to church.

"I understand this is a temporary arrangement," she continued, "because you won't need my help once you marry again."

"I know." But, if the situation had been different and he could have had his choice of wife, he would have wanted Katie. "But until then, will you help me? Take care of my children?"

She gave him a genuine smile. "*Ja*, I will watch them. Just let me know when." She turned to get out.

"Katie, hold up."

Eyes filled with curiosity, she regarded him over her shoulder.

"Wait, *sigh so gude*," he said. *Please.* "Let me help you."

Katie opened her mouth as if to object but then she surprised him by nodding without a word.

Micah hopped down and rounded his vehicle. He reached up for Katie, caught her by the waist before he gently lifted her down. He studied her and felt a longing for something that would never be. "Lie down and feel better, Katie." His tone was gentle.

She smiled at him. "*Danki* for the ride home, Micah." Then she turned and started toward the house.

He couldn't stop himself from calling her name. "Katie!"

Katie paused and faced him. *"Ja?"*

"I'll let you know when we move into the house. It may be longer than I'd hoped now that we must build the barn. My *grosseldra* will be moving here to New Berne, and my *vadder*, *bruders* and I have a *dawdi haus* to build."

She grinned at him. "Just let me know when you need me and I'll be here." She turned back to the house, halted and faced him again. "I'll see you at the barn raising on Tuesday."

Unable to help himself, he grinned back at her. "See you then." He watched her enter the house before he climbed into his wagon for the drive back to Jed's place. He felt a little better after talking with Katie. Micah hoped she was all right. He didn't like that she was feeling poorly.

He was eager to see her on Tuesday for the barn raising. He hoped that she felt well enough to attend.

His brother Jacob would have married Katie if he'd lived. Yet, he couldn't help liking her for himself…wishing for something more with the lovely woman whose allegiance was to a man who was no longer alive to marry her.

Her heart was racing as Katie entered the house. She was surprised—and pleased—by her conversation with Micah before he'd left. She went upstairs to lie down but she already felt better. His apology and the way he regarded her warmed her heart. She knew that he would marry someday, but she hoped they would still be friends, even though she wished they could be more. But Micah wouldn't be marrying for love, and she would never marry for anything else.

She entered her room and lay down on the bed. Katie felt the pinprick of tears as she thought of not being able to spend time with him, with his children. She closed her eyes and tried to conjure up Jacob's face, yet all she could see was Micah's. Guilt hit her hard, but there was nothing she could do about her feelings for Micah.

She would take each day as it came. Tomorrow she'd make food for the barn raising to ensure that the workers were well fed. And she would talk with Uri about helping Micah with the *dawdi haus* and Micah's.

She tried not to think about Naomi and the match she'd make for Micah. It hurt too much. Sleep eluded her, and her stomach burn came back with a vengeance.

Whatever happened would be *Gott's* will, and she must accept the fact that her life hadn't turned out as she'd hoped it would.

Please, Lord, keep me strong in the days ahead. Days when everything between Micah and me will change.

Chapter Thirteen

"That's going up faster than I thought," Betty said as she eyed the nearly completed new barn.

Katie's mother put a plate of brownies on the table for the men to enjoy when they took their break. "Everyone turned out to help. Members of our community are always there for each other."

Katie didn't comment. She was too busy watching and worrying about Micah who knelt high up on the roof trusses, setting plywood and nailing it. If he fell from that height... Her heart stopped when his brothers Jonathan and Vernon climbed up on two ladders, carrying a plywood sheet between them. Micah reached for it and helped his brothers slide it into place before he hammered it down. She watched nervously for a time then had to turn away.

"Katie." She spun to find her mother studying her thoughtfully.

She managed to smile. "*Ja*, Mam?" A brisk breeze blew in, making her hug herself as she shot another nervous glance toward the roof.

"They'll be fine. They're about finished with the plywood."

Katie nodded. "I don't like them up there. The wind has picked up." She felt her mother's touch on her shoulder. The framework was done. Her brothers Uri and Joseph along with her father had installed metal siding across one side of the structure. Would it hold in this wind? Her gaze returned to Micah. She wanted him—and his brothers—to get down safely before there was a terrible accident.

"Dochter." Her *mam* pointed toward the barn. "See! They're coming down now. Looks like the only thing left to be done is the metal roof and the rest of the siding. I'm sure they'll wait until the weather is more cooperative before they finish it."

"I hope you're right," Katie murmured, her gaze fixated on Micah, the one man she'd been unable to put out of her mind. The wind had calmed a bit, but she didn't trust that it wouldn't return.

"Let's finish putting out the food," Mam said. "I'm sure the workers will want a snack to hold them over until supper."

"Do you think we should keep the food inside?" Katie asked.

"Nay, I doubt Betty will want them traipsing through the house, trailing sawdust and who knows what else on her floor." She glanced at the food table, apparently satisfied by what she saw. She gestured toward a five-gallon water jug. "Katie, will you check to see if that is full?"

"I will, Mam." Katie checked the jug and saw that there was plenty of water. She wished she'd thought to make enough iced tea or lemonade to fill it, but water was probably best for thirsty men.

She brought out the two dried apple pies she'd made yesterday then placed them on the table. She had baked all Monday morning so that she could bring a huge pan of brownies, two apple pies and two chocolate cakes that the men had snapped up earlier with pleased expressions on their faces. She hid a smile. At least Micah had grinned as he'd enjoyed a piece of the chocolate cake earlier. He'd sat on one of the chairs that she had carried outside for whenever the workers took breaks.

A gust rose, catching hold of a stack of paper plates and sending them soaring across the yard. Katie grabbed what she could, but then she had to chase after the rest as they skittered across the lawn. Several times as she stretched for one, the breeze moved it out of reach. She managed to step on one and caught another. As she picked up the one under her foot, she sensed someone kneel down close by to snag those she couldn't capture. She glanced up to thank the person and inhaled sharply when she saw it was Micah. With several plates in one hand, he grinned at her as he stood and helped her to her feet.

"Here you go," he said, his voice husky and warm. "I don't know if you should use these."

She nodded. "We can't. *Danki.*" Katie felt her face heat as she accepted the paper plates he'd collected for her. A strong blast of air grabbed her *kapp*, stripping it from her head. *"Ach nay! Meim kapp!"* She gasped and pressed a hand to her head as the continuing wind tugged on her hair, freeing numerous strands from their pins. Alarmed, she met his gaze. His lips twitched before he chased down her head covering and returned it to her.

"Danki," she murmured, feeling shy under the intensity of his gaze.

Another gust blew, taking Katie by surprise, making her stumble. Micah reached out to steady her. "We can't control the weather, Katie," he said with a touch of humor.

She blinked. Was he flirting with her? "I know."

He released her with a smirk. She gaped at him, startled, as he caught her hand and tugged her to the food table. "What treats do we have here?"

Buzzing from his grasp, she pulled away. Katie didn't care for his expression as he studied her with gleaming blue eyes and an odd little smile on his very masculine lips. Was he mocking her? Or teasing her?

She studied him. Teasing her, she thought with amusement. Micah wouldn't willingly hurt her feelings. Their discussion and his understanding when he drove her home after church service assured her of what type of man he was. *A* gut *man.*

A blast of high wind threatened the table. "Maybe get everything inside," Micah suggested as he reached for the pie that had slid to the edge of the table.

"Ja." She picked up the brownies and the remainder of the chocolate cake. "Betty! Mam!" she called. "We're going to get these desserts inside out of the wind!"

Katie started toward the house, then paused to

look back. Micah was right behind her, carrying her two dried apple pies. "Mam didn't think your *mudder* would want the workers inside," she said.

"My *mam* raised five strapping sons. A little dirt or sawdust doesn't bother her." He rubbed a hand across the back of his neck.

Katie nodded, sadly aware that Jacob had been one of them. "You're not going back up on the roof today, are you?"

"*Nay*. We'll wait until the weather is better suited."

Relieved, she smiled at him before she continued into the house.

A burst of wind rattled the installed metal siding. She glanced back toward the barn. "Is the siding going to hold?"

Micah narrowed his gaze as he checked the integrity of the siding. "Hope so. If not, I guess we'll have to redo it. I don't want anyone or anything hurt if it goes."

As they climbed the two steps, Micah's sister Addie opened the door for them and took the pies from her brother. Micah went back outside. Katie placed the desserts on the kitchen table and looked through the window to see that Betty and her mother had picked up the rest of the food while the men, including Micah, were grabbing chairs and tables to store out of the wind. She saw her brother Uri coming out of the structure with a hammer and boxes of nails.

Several minutes later, Uri entered the house, grinning. "Stuck the tools on the front porch in the corner," he told Micah as they walked in together.

Micah smiled. *"Danki.* Just have to finish the siding and the metal roof and then we'll be done."

Uri nodded. His brown eyes flickered to his sister. "Katie, Dat said we'll be heading home in about an hour."

"Oll recht," she said without meeting Micah's gaze. Katie enjoyed spending time with him. More than she should. He'd been helpful today, and she couldn't seem to get him—and this sweet side of him—out of her mind. Soon, she'd be babysitting at his new house. She loved his little ones, and it didn't hurt that she might be able to spend more time with their father.

Micah's fifteen-year-old sister approached. Emma had returned to New Berne yesterday afternoon with her brother and grandparents, who now lived in the main house until a *dawdi haus* could be built on the property. The teenager had spent most of the day inside with Micah's children. "Katie, Micah's *kinner* and I loved your chocolate cake," Emma gushed. "It was so moist and delicious. Chocolate is my favorite."

Katie smiled. "I'm glad you all enjoyed it. Are the little ones asleep?"

"Ja, I just put them down."

"Emma, you didn't eat all of the dessert, *schweschter,* did you?" Micah teased.

His sister grinned. "And what if I did?"

Micah moved to go after her, and Emma shrieked and laughingly scooted out of reach. Watching them, Katie chuckled.

She was setting out plates when her mother approached. "Katie, your *kapp*," she murmured for her ears alone.

"*Ach nay!* Sorry, Mam," she exclaimed, but her mother only smiled and gestured toward the great room with a nod of her head. Embarrassed, Katie hurried and did the best she could putting her head covering back on. It wasn't easy, given the state of her wind-tousled hair. She felt self-conscious as she rejoined the others until she saw the men smiling and heard them chatting as they filled the Bontragers' family dinner plates with the desserts she'd made.

After everyone had eaten, her mother washed the dishes while Katie dried them. Micah's mother and sisters put away the leftover food and wiped down the kitchen table and counters.

Soon, with the kitchen cleaned and dishes put away, Katie was on her way home with her family, empty plates on her lap. Reflecting, she decided it had been a good day. Micah had teased and flirted with her, which made her giddy. And for the first time in a long time, she realized that she hadn't been so consumed with Jacob's memory that she couldn't enjoy the day…or her interactions with his older brother.

A week had passed since the barn raising. Katie hadn't been back to the Bontragers, but she knew the barn was complete. She'd heard the news from Uri, who had helped Micah and his brothers with the metal roof and siding. It hadn't been the type of day that involved feeding the community so there'd been no reason for Katie to go, except to see Micah, which would be awkward given their circumstances.

"Gabriel and Levi brought back Evan's livestock," Uri said conversationally as the family ate lunch together. "The new barn is bigger than the old one. There's plenty of room for more animals if Evan wants them." He grinned. "We ordered the lumber for the *dawdi haus* for Betty's *eldra*. I'm going to build it with Micah and his *bruders*. Betty insists Micah finish his *haus* renovations first. Micah agreed, said it would be best for his family if he moved into his own home with his *kinner*."

Katie felt a flutter in her chest as she anticipated Micah's move. She'd be babysitting again once they lived in the new house, and she looked forward to spending time with Jacob, Rebecca and Eliza...and their father. "Are you going to help him with the renovations?"

"*Ja*, I'm going to refinish his wood floors." Uri took a bite of fried chicken. "Micah wants to install vinyl in the children's rooms. I'm going to help him with that, too."

"*Gut,*" Dat said. "I'm sure he'll appreciate it."

Katie regarded her brother with affection. "I'm sure he'll be pleased for your help, *bruder*."

She longed to see the progress Micah made on his house, but she knew it would seem odd if she showed up unannounced when she had no reason to be in the area.

"The outbuilding is too small on Micah's property." Uri forked up a mouthful of mashed potatoes. "Micah told me that there is no hurry with a barn, as he only has his two horses. He plans to purchase livestock in the spring."

"I know he's worried about making sure his *gros-seldra* have enough room." Mam passed her husband the bowl of buttered corn. "Betty told me Micah is sharing a room with all of his *kinner*."

Katie could only imagine how tight the quarters were in Micah's room with himself and his three little ones. "I'm sure everything will work out in the end," she said, and her family agreed.

"How is Betty's *vadder*?" Dat asked.

Mam handed a bowl of peas to her youngest son. "Weak, Betty said. He's been having problems with his legs since he fell. Betty is going to take him to a doctor here in New Berne."

"That's wise." Katie watched Abraham spoon the green vegetable onto his plate.

The family spoke of other things as they ate their lunch. Her father wanted to buy a new plow, but it would have to wait. He'd need to use the old one until money was available for the purchase. Katie thought about the money she'd been putting aside from her sewing work. She had given some of it to her *mam* to contribute to the household. She could afford to give Dat money toward the new plow and could make do without savings for a while. It wasn't as if she had to move out of the house next month. Katie would keep enough for any sewing supplies she'd need to continue with her business.

When lunch was done, Katie cleaned up with her mother and sisters and then went to her room. She'd sewed each day since the barn raising and was thrilled after learning that several customers had requested her services through Kings General Store. Two days ago she'd picked up several more bags of items that needed mending. Katie decided to make Emma a new dress to replace the one she'd borrowed on the day of the fire.

She smiled. Emma was the Bontrager sibling who looked most like her oldest brother. With bright blue eyes like Micah's and features much the same, Emma could be considered the feminine version of him. The only other difference was her hair color, which was a much darker shade than Micah's light brown.

She had finished her mending work that morning and was nearly done with Emma's dress. Katie decided to make deliveries to her customers' homes this afternoon before returning to the house to complete the last bit of stitching on Emma's clothing.

As she made the trip toward her last stop, Katie realized that she would have to pass by Micah's house. She recalled the first day she'd met him. She'd been so shocked to see someone who looked so much like Jacob, her late fiancé, that she had almost passed out. Fortunately, she had come to know Micah and was well over the shock now. His personality was nothing like Jacob's. The brothers' features and mannerisms might be similar, but Micah was taller, his presence more commanding and it was clear that he was the older of the two.

She was eager to see the house. It would be all right if she stopped, wouldn't it? It wasn't as if she had driven over just to see the progress. She was making deliveries and she still had one left. No one would think anything of it if she stopped to say *hallo* and to see what he'd done.

It was a beautiful day for a ride in her pony cart. Fall had come upon them, and bright red-and-green apples hung on trees in Beiler's Orchard as she rode past. She considered buying some fresh apples, but then decided she would come back to shop another day. Apple season had just begun, and there was plenty of time.

Micah's house was ahead and to the right. She waited for a car to pass from behind her before she made the turn onto Micah's driveway. She parked, eager to see his house—and him. There was another vehicle in the driveway so she stopped close to the road. It didn't look like Uri's, but maybe one of Micah's own brothers had come over to help him.

Katie got out and started toward the house when the side door opened and two women stepped out— one older and a much younger woman with auburn hair and lovely features. Katie recognized the older woman as the matchmaker, Naomi Hostetler. She froze as she realized Naomi must have found a match for Micah. While Katie watched with a sinking feeling in her chest, the women climbed into a buggy. Micah came out of the house and waved at them from the steps as they left.

Heart pumping hard, stomach burning with pain, Katie could only gaze at Micah, the man, she suddenly realized, she had fallen for hard, despite her attempts to convince herself that she only wanted to be his friend. If he were just her friend, she wouldn't be feeling this heartbreak. She spun and climbed into her pony cart, eager to get away before he saw her.

"Katie!" he called out.

She inhaled sharply and kept going. Ignoring Micah calling her name, she drove away from the house and the man she loved. She was hurt and angry. Apparently, he planned to be married soon; yet, he hadn't told her he no longer needed her.

Struggling against tears, Katie made her last delivery but didn't stay to chat. When she got home, she ran up to her room where she lay on the bed and allowed herself to cry. Finally dry eyed, she got up and went to work adding the final touches to Emma's dress with a painful lump in her throat.

"Katie." Her mother entered her room.

Katie didn't immediately respond. She pressed on the sewing machine pedal and ran stitches down one seam.

"Dochter." Mam's tone was firm.

She blinked up at her. *"Ja,* Mam*?"*

"What's wrong?"

"Nothing, Mam. I'm fine." She started sewing again. "Just busy trying to get this dress done and one other order that came in through Kings."

Her mother didn't say anything, but she didn't leave either. When Katie stayed silent, Mam sighed then left.

Katie stopped the sewing machine and hung her head, trying not to cry. Micah was getting married and she'd lost something special. She loved the man and he would wed that other young, pretty woman, leaving Katie to continue with her plans to make a living from her sewing.

* * *

Micah watched Katie climb into her vehicle and leave. She wouldn't look at him. He didn't understand why she stopped but didn't stay to visit. And then suddenly he realized that she must have seen Naomi and Iris as they left.

She's upset because she believes I no longer need her to babysit.

He would have to explain to Katie that it wasn't the case. He had planned to tell her about the finished house later this afternoon and that he would be moving in by the end of the next week. He needed—and wanted—her to watch his children for him again. He'd been excited at the prospect of seeing Katie in his newly renovated house.

He frowned. Did she have so little faith in him that she was quick to believe he wouldn't talk with her first to tell her he was marrying?

Closing his eyes, Micah tried not to be angry with her. He cared for her, more than he should since the only thing Katie was willing to give him was her babysitting services—and her friendship.

Nay, he couldn't be angry. Katie had looked distraught, and it bothered him to see her so upset. He would have to find out why she seemed hurt so that he could repair their friendship...

And if he had anything to do with it—he would seek to find out if there was a possibility of something more with her.

Chapter Fourteen

Emma Bontrager visited Katie two days after she saw Naomi leaving Micah's house with the young woman. "Mam wants you to come for tea. She would have extended the invitation herself," the teenager said, "but she doesn't want to leave my *grosseldra*."

Katie knew that Betty worried about her parents, especially her father. "How is your *grossdaddi*?"

Emma toyed with her *kapp* string. "He doesn't have good use of his legs which frustrates him, but otherwise he seems *oll recht*. He eats and sleeps well."

"I hope they find the answer to his problem soon."

"*Ja*, I do, too," Emma said. "So, will you come over for tea? I know you're probably busy, but Mam would love it if you could."

Katie didn't want to visit the Bontragers because of Micah, the last person she wanted to see. But she couldn't deny his mother, who'd been nothing but kind and loving toward her since the day her new beau Jacob had brought her home to meet his parents and share a meal. At the time, the Bontragers were recent additions to New Berne and her Amish community. Katie had met Jacob after he'd come to a singing at the invitation of their neighbor, a young man close to Jacob's age.

"*Ja*, Emma. I'll be there. What time?"

Emma blushed. "Can you come now?"

"*Oll recht.*" Katie managed to smile. "But can you wait a moment? I have something I want to get for you. Let me just run upstairs, then I'll follow you to your *haus*."

Katie hurried up the stairs to retrieve Emma's new dress from her bedroom. She'd chosen a beautiful shade of purple, a color that went well with Emma's pretty blue eyes. And she knew the teenager would love the cheerfully bright color.

When she returned to the kitchen, she saw that her brother Uri had come in from outside. He and Emma stood in the kitchen in silence. Uri appeared uncomfortable but couldn't take his eyes off the lovely girl. Emma barely looked at him and apparently had nothing to say to him. The tension between them seemed thick and painful. Katie hesitated in the doorway before making herself known as she entered the room.

"Here we are, Emma!" Katie announced loudly, breaking the awkward silence. She pretended to be surprised to see her brother. "Uri! I'm so glad you're home, *bruder*! I'm running low on baking supplies, and I wondered if you'd do me a big favor and pick them up for me."

She saw Uri reluctantly drag his gaze from Emma to focus on his sister. Katie glimpsed a sadness in his lovesick brown eyes, and she wished she could do something to ease his pain. *"Ja.* What do you need?"

After fetching a list of items she'd wanted for baking from a kitchen drawer, she handed it to him. She smiled when he took it from her. *"Danki, bruder."*

His eyes fell on Micah's sister. "Emma," he murmured with a nod and then he left.

The girl's expression as she followed Uri longingly with her eyes as he left the house was telling. Katie hid a smile. The teenager clearly liked Uri but didn't know how to interact with him. "Emma."

The girl blinked. *"Ja?"*

Katie gave her a soft smile. "I borrowed your dress after the fire. Mine was ruined…and well… I'm afraid yours is too since I did a quick washup and couldn't take a shower. I'm sorry but I haven't been able to clean it for you. So, I made this. I know it isn't the same color as the one I borrowed…" She held up the new dress to show Emma.

"Purple!" Emma exclaimed as she reached to finger the fabric. "I love it!" She frowned as if something suddenly occurred to her. "Katie, you didn't have to go to all this trouble. I don't care if my dress is ruined. You didn't have to replace it." She smiled and her expression was soft as she studied her new garment with glistening blue eyes. "It's such a beautiful dress," she said with reverence. "I've never had one like it." She sniffed as she met Katie's gaze. *"Danki*, Katie. I can't wait to wear it. When I do, I'm going to tell everyone that you made it for me."

Katie shifted uncomfortably. "You don't have to do that."

Emma bobbed her head. "*Ja*, I do." She accepted the dress from Katie. "Mam said that you're a seamstress. If I wear this and tell them about you, you may get new customers."

Nodding, Katie realized that the girl had a point. She hadn't done it because she wanted recognition but simply because she owed Emma a dress. If someone wanted her to make a dress for them, she'd be happy to do so. After all, she wanted to sew for living. Didn't she?

Emma insisted that Katie ride with her when it was time to leave. "You don't need to drive over, Katie. I have to run an errand later, and I'll be heading past your house when I do."

Katie decided not to argue and agreed. How could she fault Emma's logic? She said a silent prayer that Micah wouldn't be home while she was there.

Ten minutes later, Emma pulled close to the Bontrager house. Betty opened the door as the girls got out of the pony cart and approached. "Katie!" Micah's mother greeted. "It is *gut* to see you! It seems too long since we chatted."

Katie smiled. She wondered why Betty was so eager to have her to tea.

"Mam, look at this dress!" Grinning, Emma held up the new garment. "Katie made it for me!"

"She did?" Betty was clearly surprised. "That was kind of you, Katie."

"I borrowed one of hers after the fire. Emma's size was the closest to mine." She blushed, remembering how Micah had grabbed a dress out of Emma's room for her so she could wash up a bit and then change before they rode with Bert to pick up his children. "Mine is ruined," she explained, feeling awkward.

"I'm sorry to hear that." The older woman eyed her with affection.

"I tried to clean Emma's, but I can't get all of the soot and mud out."

Betty shuddered, no doubt thinking of the fire. "Every time I think of you and Micah in that barn…"

"It was frightening," Katie said as she thought about what it would have been like if Micah hadn't arrived when he had. She would have been alone in a burning barn. Would she have been able to save Evan's livestock?

With Micah's name coming into their conversation, she wanted to ask Betty about the woman who was with the matchmaker, the one her son planned to marry. But she didn't. She knew it would hurt too much to learn about Micah's future wife—and the family's pleasure in their son's upcoming wedding.

"Please, Katie. Sit down," Betty invited.

Katie pulled out a kitchen chair and took a seat as Emma poured each of them tea.

"Cookies?" Emma asked, and her mother nodded.

"I hope you like chocolate chip."

Katie smiled. "I do."

"How is your *mudder*?" Betty asked.

"She's doing fine. Been busy. She bought apples to put up. Abigail and Ruthann are going to help her when she's ready." Katie took a sip of tea. "How are your *eldra*, Betty? Emma said that your *vadder* is eating and sleeping well. Is he any better?"

"Nay." The older woman sighed. "He's still the

same. I made an appointment for him to get his legs checked. We have no idea why he's still having trouble with them. I can only hope and pray that the doctor will shed some light on his problem. And that something can be done."

"I have faith that you'll find an answer soon," she said softly.

"My parents are managing by sleeping downstairs, but it will be *gut* for them to have their own *haus*. Their place in Indiana is up for sale. The Realtor thinks it will sell quickly."

"That would be a blessing," Katie agreed.

Unable to help herself, Katie wondered about the progress on Micah's house. Was it finished? Uri hadn't been home much lately and she hadn't wanted to ask when he didn't offer the information.

"I will continue to have faith that Dat will get better and my *eldra* will be happy here in New Berne."

"I'm sure they will." Katie sipped her tea. "They have you and your family, and our community will do everything we can to help."

"They will, Mam," Emma said. "*Grossdaddi* and *grossmammi* wanted to move here."

Betty smiled at her daughter. Then the woman focused her gaze on Katie with a thoughtful expression that made Katie slightly uncomfortable. "I have a favor to ask."

"Ja?" She hoped the favor had nothing to do with Micah.

"I have a great deal of mending to be done, and since my parents moved here, I haven't had the time."

"Mam, I can do it for you," Emma offered.

"*Nay*, Emma. You've seen Katie's ability to sew in your new dress," Betty said with a glance toward the garment. "I'd like Katie to do this for me, if she will." She gave Emma an affectionate smile to soften the sting before she returned her attention to Katie. "I'll pay you the going rate."

"Betty, I'll do it, but you don't have to pay me—"

"*Ja*, I do. Please. Just knowing that you're willing to do this for me is such a blessing."

Katie nodded. *"Oll recht."* She watched as Betty stood up and left the room. Micah's mother returned within minutes carrying a large wicker basket of clothing. Katie stood and took it from her. "You didn't have to invite me to tea to ask for my help. Emma could have just dropped it off."

"I wanted to visit with you, Katie. I feel as if we don't see enough of you these days."

"I'm sorry, Betty. I don't mean to keep *meim* distance."

"Will you be going to the preacher's *haus* for Visiting Day?" Betty asked a half hour later when Katie got up to leave after Emma said she was ready to run her errand and take Katie home. It had been a lovely afternoon. Except for a short conversation about the fire, the subject of Micah hadn't been discussed.

"Mam mentioned spending time with her *schweschter* on Sunday."

"Ah well, then have a *wunderbor* time. Don't be a stranger."

"I won't," Katie promised. *"Danki* for the tea and cookies." Emma had plated delicious homemade chocolate chip cookies for Katie to take home.

"You're *willkomm*." The woman smiled as she walked Katie to the door.

As she followed Emma outside, Katie heard metal buggy wheels on the driveway.

"Micah," Emma greeted.

"Schweschter," he said, sounding amused.

Alarmed, Katie stole a quick glance in his direction and encountered the intensity of his bright blue gaze. She quickly averted her eyes. Katie tried to act as if she wasn't affected by Micah's presence as she prayed silently that he wouldn't address her directly. Since the day she'd seen Naomi and the pretty young woman leave his house, she'd felt vulnerable—and hurt. She knew she had no reason to feel that way. It wasn't as if they were in a relationship. She only wished they were.

Since then, however, she'd managed to avoid him. He would marry the young woman Naomi had found for him, and he'd marry not for love but to provide a new mother for his children. *But what if he falls in love with her?* She swallowed against a painful lump. Micah had captured her heart, but given the circumstances, there was nothing for her to do except try to get past her feelings for him.

"How is the *haus* coming along?" she heard Emma ask.

Micah smiled. *"Gut.* It won't be long before we can move."

"We love having you all here with us," his sister said with a frown.

"You know it's better for everyone if we move. It's not far. You can visit whenever you like."

Her heart picked up the pace as she attempted to slip by unnoticed toward Emma's vehicle with the wicker basket in her arms. When it was silent, Katie paused to check whether Emma was following, but there was no sign of the girl.

"If you're looking for my sister, she apparently forgot something in the house." Micah had approached, and he was so close she could smell his soap and a pleasant outdoorsy scent that only belonged to him. "Let me help you with that."

Katie met his gaze, and the warmth in his blue eyes made her catch her breath. "Your *mudder* asked me to tea," she said, feeling suddenly shy as she allowed him to take the basket.

He carried it and set it on the ground next to the cart before he extended his hand to her. Katie hesitated. She wanted to clasp that strong hand, feel the warmth of his fingers surrounding hers. But she knew that the moment their hands touched, she'd be lost.

Ignoring his outstretched hand, Katie reached up to grab hold of the side to hoist herself in. With a growl of frustration, Micah startled her when he grabbed her waist from behind and lifted her into the vehicle. He picked up the basket and handed it to her.

"Danki," she murmured, meeting his gaze, but it was as if a shutter had closed over his features, effectively shielding his thoughts. Without another word, he started to walk away. "Micah!"

He froze and then faced her.

"I wish you every happiness," she said softly, fighting tears.

His expression softened. "Katie, we need to talk—"

"Ready to go?" Emma exclaimed, interrupting.

"I'm ready when you are," Katie said, tearing her gaze from the man who was constantly in her thoughts.

"*Bruder*, tell Mam I won't be long," his sister said happily. "After I take Katie home, I have a quick errand to run."

"Be careful," Micah said, his deep voice drawing Katie's attention. He had spoken to his sister but his gaze was locked on Katie. The concern in his eyes for her warmed her heart.

Katie rewarded him with a genuine smile. "Take care of yourself, Micah," she said as Emma climbed onto the side and picked up the leathers. "Give your *kinner* a hug from me."

Emma drove the cart away, leaving Katie wishing things were different, that he wanted her—not as simply a woman as a mother for his children, but as the woman he wanted to marry because he loved her.

Micah couldn't stop thinking about Katie. It seemed like forever since he'd seen her. Today was Visiting Day at the preacher's house. David Bontrager was a distant cousin on his father's side of the family. Would Katie and her family be visiting there today? He hoped so. He wanted to talk with her, find out what had upset her, see if he could help in any way. Did it have something to do with Naomi and Iris's visit? He frowned. Surely, she didn't believe that Naomi had found him a wife. *Nay.* Katie must know that he would tell her if his circumstances changed.

He pulled his suspenders over his shoulders and clipped them in place. He had dressed Jacob, and with his sisters' help, Eliza and Rebecca were ready for the outing as well. Micah ran a comb through his hair before he went downstairs. He really hoped he'd get to see Katie today.

"Are you ready to go?" his father asked.

"Ja." Micah looked around. "Where are my youngsters?"

"Outside with your sisters," his brother Jonathan said as he entered the house.

"It would be nice seeing everyone, but I think I should stay home with my *eldra*," Mam said.

"Why can't they come with us?" Micah asked. "They traveled by car here from Indiana, and they did fine, *ja*?"

"Ja," his mother conceded. "They did."

"Why don't I take *Grossdaddi* and *Grossmammi* and you take Eliza and Rebecca?"

"That sounds like a fine plan," his grandmother said as she moved into the room. "Betty, your *dat* will be right here. He may have trouble with his legs, but he wants to go. He is tired of being cooped up inside."

"Truth," his grandfather said as Matthew and Vernon helped him into a kitchen chair. "I may have not *gut* use of my legs, but I have my faculties. With my *grosssoohn*'s help, I'll get to visit. You can put me in a chair there and go about your business. I'm sure I'll find someone to talk to."

His mother looked apologetic. "Dat, I don't mean to keep you from everyone." She moved closer to touch her father's shoulder. "I just worry about you, but if you want to go, we'll make sure you get there." She glanced toward her oldest son.

"*Ja*, I'll make sure you get there safely," Micah said with a smile.

Less than an hour later, the Bontrager and Yoder families were on their way to David Bontrager's house. Micah's grandfather, Elmer Yoder, sat beside his grandson in Micah's family buggy. Elmer's wife, Mae, Micah's grandmother, was in the backseat with little Jacob and Matthew, Micah's brother.

His grandfather seemed comfortable and lighter in spirit since they'd left the house. It wasn't far to the preacher's property, and before long Micah made the turn and pulled onto David's driveway. There were already buggies parked along the left side of the barn. Micah parked on the end closest to the road so that he could leave if his grandfather got too tired to stay.

Micah climbed down from the buggy then skirted the vehicle to help Matthew with their grandfather. "*Grossdaddi*, do you think we should get you a wheelchair?" Matt asked.

"*Nay!* I can walk," Elmer said. "I haven't seen the doctor yet, and I'll not be giving up anytime soon."

Micah's father drove into the lot with the rest of the family. He parked on the farthest side of the line of buggies, no doubt understanding why Micah parked where he did.

After Matt took care of their grandfather, Micah helped his grandmother from the carriage. Jacob hopped out behind her and held on to Grandmother Mae's hand. Micah couldn't help smiling at his son. He turned to his brother.

"Matt, can you find a chair for him?"

His brother nodded and took off, running toward the house and the gathering of men outside. Micah saw him talking with the preacher, who glanced briefly in their direction. David nodded and then retrieved a chair from the front porch, setting it close to the circle of men who were more than happy to include Elmer in their conversation as soon as he was situated.

Naomi Hostetler arrived with Iris, the young woman who had come to visit from his former Amish village in Michigan. Micah helped his mother and sisters carry the food toward the house. After he'd relinquished the dishes into his sister Emma's capable hands, he turned to see where Naomi and Iris had gone. He'd known Iris for many years. He was surprised and pleased to see her.

Another vehicle pulled onto the property. Micah was stunned to see Mervin Mast and his family, as his mother had mentioned that the Masts wouldn't be visiting the preacher today. A few minutes later, he became alert as Katie came into view, carrying a large metal pan. Wondering what delicious dessert she'd made, he smiled. It was good to see her. He'd have to find time to talk with her. He would be moving soon, and he needed to know if she was still willing to watch his son and daughters for him.

"Micah!" Uri called out to him as he followed with his brothers behind his sisters.

Micah saw Katie stiffen and briefly glance his way. She was clearly unhappy to see him. He frowned. The question was why? As he moved to speak with her brother, he decided he would find out exactly why she was avoiding him when he thought they'd become, at least, friends.

Micah was here. Katie struggled to take deep, calming breaths as she walked toward the house, knowing that he watched her. She'd thought they were going to visit her mother's sister for Visiting Day, but she found out only this morning that her parents had changed their minds and decided they would visit Preacher David today instead. Fortunately, Katie had baked a huge pan of bread pudding to bring to her aunt's and a batch of whoopie pies for the family to enjoy during the week. Now she carried the bread pudding while her sister Abigail carried the large tray of whoopie pies.

She entered the house with Abigail behind her.

"Katie!" Betty exclaimed, the first to see her. "You're here!"

Katie smiled. "*Ja*, Mam and Dat decided to come here instead of Mam's *schweschter*'s."

"I'm glad you could make it."

"I am nearly finished with your mending. I can drop everything by next week. Will that be soon enough?"

"*Ja*, of course, Katie," Betty said, looking pleased. "I'm surprised you can get through it so quickly."

Katie's mother entered the house with a bowl of cold baked beans. "Betty," she greeted with a smile.

"Sarah, I'm glad to see you," her mother's friend, Micah's mother, said. "It's been a while since we last visited."

"Wasn't it only two weeks ago when they came to our *haus* for Visiting Day?" Betty's son Vernon said with dry humor as he heard the last of the conversation when he entered the house.

"*Ja*, but we used to get together more during the week." Betty flashed Vernon a look that scolded. "What do you need, *soohn*?"

"Some iced tea for Grossvadder. He said he's thirsty."

"I'll be happy to get it for him," Arleta Bontrager, the preacher's wife, offered as she approached.

"*Danki*," Vernon and his mother said simultaneously and then they chuckled. Amused, Katie joined in, grinning and laughing softly.

Katie's sister Abigail entered the house. "Naomi Hostetler's here and she asked me to bring this in." She carried a large foil-covered tray.

Katie stiffened. "What is it?"

"Cream puffs," Abigail said. "I took a peek and they looked *wunderbor*."

"I'm surprised that Naomi went to all that trouble."

"I don't think she did," Katie's sister said. "Apparently, Iris made them."

Betty smiled and nodded. "*Ja*, Iris is a *gut* cook."

Her spirits plummeting fast, Katie excused herself and went outside. So that girl Iris—was she the one she saw with Naomi at Micah's? Her eyes felt scratchy as she left the house and headed toward the barn. She thought of her and Micah trapped together during the storm in his father's barn, when he'd brought her a blanket because she was shivering. She couldn't forget the way he tenderly wrapped it around her shoulders. When they'd worked together to get the livestock out of the burning building, Katie recalled his concern for her safety. He'd sounded worried, frantic. But she couldn't leave any of the animals inside to die, so had kept going until she'd felt Micah grab hold of her hand and pull her from the building. Memories of that day sent image after image into her mind. The horror of the fire was real. But being there with Micah...she'd realized that she wanted a second chance at love. With Micah. But it was too late for that. Micah had someone else now.

Katie fought tears as she entered the preacher's barn for a few moments alone. She walked slowly down its length, stopping every so often to say *hallo* to the animals that remained in their stalls. No one knew where she'd gone, but that was fine. No one would miss her. *He* wouldn't miss her.

She slid open the back barn door and exited the building. She saw a small patch of grass and sat, uncaring of possible grass stains on her sky-blue dress.

Katie wiped her eyes. She should be happy. It was a glorious sunny day, and she was finally finding peace over the loss of Jacob, her betrothed. Closing her eyes, she prayed for strength. Katie would always miss Jacob, but she knew he was happy in the house of the Lord. *Ja*, he had died too soon, but *Gott* must have had a reason to bring him home.

She didn't know how long she sat there. It hurt to

realize that Micah had found a wife, but she would go on living as she had always done. Katie stood, brushed off the back of her dress and reentered the barn. She went back the way she came until she was out in the yard.

Mam and the other women were putting out food. Katie felt guilty for not returning sooner to help them. She approached her mother. "Where have you been, *dochter*?"

"I was looking in the barn, visiting with the animals. I'm sorry I'm late. What can I do to help?"

"You can help by bringing out the desserts," Mam said quietly as if disappointed with her as she set a huge container of potato salad on the food table.

"Mam—"

"You can bring out whatever is left," Mam said firmly as she rearranged things on the table to make more room.

"*Ja*, Mam," Katie said sadly, feeling chastised. She turned to obey.

"Katie."

Katie stopped and looked back. Her mother took a long time to study her, and whatever she saw on her daughter's face softened her expression. "Are you *oll recht*?"

Katie shrugged. "I'll be fine," she said as she continued toward the house.

The screen door opened as Katie climbed the steps. The young woman she'd seen with Naomi at Micah's place came out of the house, carrying Katie's whoopie pies. Micah's future wife smiled at her. She had auburn hair and green eyes. And she was extremely pretty. Katie could only imagine the beautiful children they'd have together. Excusing herself quickly, Katie entered the house and took a moment to just breathe. Once she'd regained her composure, she grabbed a basket of cookies and fruit, the only items left in the house, and returned outside. She saw Micah talking with Uri. The two men got along well together. Katie watched Emma approach them, and with a few words for Micah, she pulled Uri away.

Katie grinned. Judging from the interaction between the couple, she realized that Uri must have told the girl that he had feelings for her. Emma smiled up at him, and Uri returned her grin. Katie's gaze settled on the man she loved just as Iris headed in his direction with a big smile on her face. Micah spied her and flashed her a grin. Katie set the desserts on the table and walked away.

She couldn't live this way. Every time she saw Micah, she would regret that she hadn't accepted Naomi's decision to match her with him. *But I wasn't ready.*

Katie realized that she would have to move on and find a life of her own. Single and alone while sewing for a living no longer seemed enough for her. She drew a sharp breath then released it.

If I can't have a life with Micah Bontrager, maybe I can have one with someone else.

Chapter Fifteen

The men were seated at tables. Katie made her way down the length of each one with an iced tea pitcher in hand, pouring refills. Iris was offering her tray of cream puffs to each of the men. At the next table, Katie watched her offer the tray to Micah and his smile as he grabbed one of the desserts.

"These look delicious," she heard him tell Iris. "I may have to go back for more."

"Why don't you take some now?" Iris suggested with what Katie considered a flirty grin.

Micah shook his head. "*Danki*, but there are other desserts I need to have."

"Are you offering a refill?" a young handsome man asked Katie from the far end of the table. He didn't look much older than she was.

"*Ja*, sorry." Katie reached for his cup and poured him iced tea. "Did you get any dessert?"

"I did. The cream puffs were delicious, but I'm partial to whoopie pies, and I saw some on the dessert table." The young man's dark eyes warmed as he smiled at her. "I'm going for one of them next."

Katie found herself smiling back. "I can bring you one if you'd like." She lowered her voice. "I made them."

"Then I definitely want one," he said with a grin, "but you don't have to serve me. I'll go grab one for myself."

Katie arched her eyebrows. "Who are you and where did you come from?" she murmured softly as she left the table, wondering why this man was unlike many other men who expected to be waited on. *Except for Micah, who is often sweet and thoughtful.* And her father.

She left the young man's table to refill the pitcher from a huge jug near the food then continued to the next dining table, the one where Micah sat. After a quick glance toward the dessert table, she saw the young man with a whoopie pie. Katie returned her focus to refilling cups with iced tea, smiling as she made her way down the table until she came to Micah.

"Micah," she mumbled, suddenly tongue-tied, as she met his gaze.

"May I have some iced tea?" he asked softly.

Nodding, she reached for his cup, and their fingers brushed as they tried for it at the same time. Katie caught her breath as she withdrew and he handed it to her. Her fingers gripping the pitcher shook a little, making it awkward as she poured his iced tea. She hoped he didn't notice. When she gave his cup back to him, he captured her attention with his warm smile. She couldn't help but smile before she started to move away.

"Katie." Micah's voice drew her back to him.

"Ja?"

"Did you make the whoopie pies?"

She nodded.

"What about the bread pudding? Do you know who made it?"

She shifted under the intensity of his bright blue gaze. "I did."

He chuckled. "I knew it."

"Is there something wrong with them?"

"Nay, they were both delicious," he said. "I could tell they were yours because everything you make always tastes so *gut.*"

Oh. "I'm glad you liked them."

Micah inclined his head, a tender smile for her teasing at his lips. *"Ja."*

She was confused. Should she thank him? Let it go? He was to marry another, but she couldn't help but be drawn to him time and again. Because Micah was a kind man. An honest man. The type of man who would make a fine husband for some fortunate woman. The moment had become suddenly awkward. *"Danki,* Micah," she said simply and continued down the table.

"Katie," Micah's voice stopped her a second time. She looked at him with confusion. His lips twitched as if he found something about her amusing. "Meet me by the barn? I need to talk with you."

"I don't know, Micah…"

"It's a *gut* thing, I promise." The look is his eyes drew her like a bear to honey.

"*Oll recht*. When?"

"Now?"

"I have to finish the refills."

"Emma!" Micah stood and waved to his sister.

"What are you doing?" Katie hissed.

Emma approached and smiled at Katie. She was wearing her new purple dress, and Katie saw that the teenager felt confident wearing it.

"*Schweschter*, would you mind helping Katie by taking over iced tea refills?"

His sister smiled. "I'll be happy to."

And Katie was forced to hand the pitcher to Emma. Once the girl left to pour tea, Micah said, "Now you can meet me by the barn."

Katie sighed dramatically. "You are a confounding man—do you know that?"

His eyes seemed to laugh at her. "I'll go first." He held up his iced tea. "I'll be there as soon as I finish this."

She didn't feel comfortable meeting Micah near the barn. Why not just have the discussion here in the yard? Still, she went to find a spot to wait for him, because Micah had asked her to—and she couldn't help herself.

He arrived a few seconds after she found a place in the rear of the barn near the preacher's pastures, eyeing the view. She sensed him immediately. He would marry another woman and she didn't have the right to spend time with him alone.

"What do you have to tell me?" He stood close, gazing down at her with a small smile on his lips.

"Ask you actually," he said. "I'll be moving into my *haus* with my *kinner* the day after tomorrow, and I was wondering if you would mind coming over to babysit for them during the day."

"You want me to watch Jacob and your girls?" she asked, surprised.

"Ja." He looked confused. "Wasn't that our arrangement?"

"Ja, but that was until you married."

"And have I married yet?"

She averted her gaze. *"Nay*, but didn't Naomi find you a wife?"

He didn't say anything at first. Sensing his hesitation, she stared up at him. "She did," he admitted softly, "but she hasn't agreed to marry me yet."

Katie felt a drop in her stomach. "I see." She cleared her throat. "You will tell me when she agrees?"

Micah held her gaze. "You'll be the first to know."

"Oke."

He sighed in apparent relief. *"Gut. Danki."*

She shrugged. "I enjoy spending time with your *soohn* and *dechter*. It's no hardship for me. They are *wunderbor kinner*." It was a pleasure to babysit for Jacob, Rebecca and Eliza, but she knew she shouldn't have gotten attached to them. But she *had* become attached.

Soon they would have a new mother to care for them, and she would no longer be needed…or be able to spend time with them. Katie turned to head to the gathering. "I should get back. I need to help with the cleanup."

Micah fell into step with her as they left the side area of the barn and approached their families and friends.

"Micah!" A big smile accompanied the feminine call as Iris beelined toward Micah.

Katie froze and she felt her face drain of color. "Micah," she said, "I'm afraid that I won't be able to watch Jacob and the girls this week."

Micah looked disappointed. "What about the following week?"

Wanting only to leave, she shook her head. "I have a lot of sewing that I almost forgot about." She managed a small smile for him. "I wish you happiness in your new *haus*, Micah." *And your new bride.*

With a sinking feeling in her chest, Katie quickly excused herself and left. She grabbed dishes along with the other women who were cleaning up and brought them into the house. She stayed inside to wrap up leftover food. Betty entered the building with Naomi. Unwilling to listen to how wonderful it was that the matchmaker had found Micah a wife, Katie put a wrapped dish in the refrigerator then left for the quiet peace of the preacher's empty great room.

"Katie." To her shock, Naomi had followed her, looking concerned. "What's wrong? How can I help?"

"Naomi, congratulations on finding a match for Micah. I'm sure he'll be very happy with her."

The matchmaker frowned. "Who?"

Katie was confused. "Micah's future wife. Iris."

The older woman smiled. "I am *gut* at making matches," she admitted. "In fact, I know someone who I think would be a good match for you, if you're interested."

Katie's immediate instinct was to say no. She meandered to a window and gazed at the gathering in the backyard. "Naomi," she said, shaking her head. Then she saw Micah talking with Iris in the yard. They stood away from the thick of the gathering, both clearly enjoying each other's company. And she made her decision. "*Oll recht.* I'll meet the man you think will be *gut* for me."

Naomi clapped her hands with excitement. "*Gut! Gut!* Come outside and I'll introduce you."

"He's here?"

"*Ja*, he's new to the area so David invited him so he would get to know members of our community. He is a *wunderbor* man. So handsome and kind!"

She followed Naomi outside. She looked at her friends and family, anywhere but where Micah and Iris stood.

"Katie, I'd like you to meet Samuel Stoltzfus. He recently moved here from New Holland."

Katie spun and was pleasantly surprised. It was the handsome man she'd served iced tea to, the man who wanted a whoopie pie.

"Samuel, this is Katie Mast."

"Ah, the woman who made the delicious whoopie pies and bread pudding," he said with a warm smile and sparkling green eyes. "It's nice to be formally introduced." He looked at Naomi. "*Danki* for this," he told her.

Naomi nodded. "Go, take a walk together. That is, if Katie is willing."

The look in Samuel's expression pleaded with her to agree.

"*Oll recht.* I'll walk with you," Katie said, "but we can't go far. I have to be ready when my *dat* says it's time to leave."

He grinned, and she couldn't help staring. Samuel truly was a handsome man. The only person who was more attractive than him was…Micah.

They started their walk toward the front yard of the preacher's house. "What made you move to New Berne?" she asked.

A long moment of silence made Katie glance up at him. There was a hint of pain in his eyes, and Katie was afraid to hear why.

"I lost *meim frau*," he admitted.

Katie closed her eyes. He'd lost his wife. *Nay*, not him, too. "I'm sorry."

"I'm fine. It was a few years ago. And just recently I made the decision to move closer to *meim bruders*, who live in New Berne."

She had so many questions and struggled to decide what to ask first. "Do you have children?"

"*Nay*, we weren't married long enough." They walked along the flower garden that Altera, David's wife, must have planted last spring. "Do you like *kinner*?"

Her soft smile. "I do."

They continued around the front of the house to the side yard. Samuel gestured toward the side entrance to a large porch that ran the full front length of the house. "Would you like to sit for a bit?"

"Sure." Katie climbed onto the porch and took a seat in a white rocker. "It's peaceful here, away from everyone." She began to rock back and forth in the chair.

"Ja." She could feel this direct gaze on her. "Tell me about you," he said. "Why aren't you married and with children?"

She looked away. "I should have been," she said softly, "but I lost my betrothed last year. Farm accident. It happened the month before we were to marry."

"Less than a year then." Samuel got quiet.

His green eyes were enhanced by his light spring-green shirt. She couldn't help but notice the thickness of the man's arms. A man who, no doubt, did physical work for a living, she thought. "Are you in construction?" she asked.

He seemed surprised by her question. *"Ja,* I am. Why do you ask?"

She blushed. "The thought just occurred that maybe you were."

"I worked for a construction company in New Holland. Not sure what I'll be doing here, though."

"Hmm. Maybe you can check with Jed King at the general store or Aaron Hostetler. They both have worked in construction. If you want to continue with that line of work, then I'd talk with them. They may be able to help you."

"That's nice of you, Katie. I'll do that."

Katie liked Samuel, but Micah was the only one

for her. While she'd never have Micah, she realized that she wasn't ready to spend time with any other man except as a friend. "Samuel, I don't know what Naomi told you about me…or if you're looking for a sweetheart or wife, but I… I can be your friend but I can't be anything else."

Samuel grinned. "To be honest, I'm not looking for anything serious. But a friend I can use."

Katie grinned and stood. "We should get back to everyone. My *dat* will be about ready to go home."

Samuel went down the stairs ahead of her and then offered his hand to help her descend the steps. As they returned to the backyard, he excused himself as Naomi made her way to Katie's side.

"How was it?" the matchmaker asked.

"Samuel is a nice man. Kind and handsome just as you said…"

"But?"

"I'm sorry, Naomi, but it isn't going to work between us. Samuel and I will be *gut* friends but nothing more."

To Katie's surprise, Naomi wasn't the least bit upset. "Tell me…how do you feel about Micah Bontrager?"

"We're neighbors. His family and mine are close friends."

The matchmaker's gaze turned shrewd. "How do *you* feel about him?" She paused. "Not as a family man but as an attractive man?"

"Naomi…"

"I know you have feelings for Micah, Katie," the older woman said.

Katie gasped and felt her face flush with heat. She knew that Naomi would see the telltale sign of Katie's bright red skin and realize that she was right. Katie did find Micah attractive, and she had fallen in love with him. "I know he'll be marrying Iris," she said.

"*Nay*, he doesn't want nor love Iris," Naomi assured her. "Iris is a friend of mine and…Micah's late wife's cousin. She is like a *schweschter* to him."

As if hearing her name, Iris approached. "Have you seen Betty?"

"I believe she's near her family's buggy." Naomi gestured toward the buggy in question. "Iris, I'd like you to meet Katie Mast. Katie, this is Iris. She is visiting from Centreville. She is friends with Micah because of a family connection with…" She stopped before she said the name, but Katie knew it was Anna, Micah's late wife.

Iris eyed her with a smile. "Katie, it's lovely to meet you."

Katie smiled back. Now that she knew Micah wasn't marrying the woman, she was happy to be friendly with her.

Iris left in search of Micah's mother, and Naomi faced Katie. The matchmaker's expression softened. "You love him. You love Micah."

Katie released a sharp breath. "I do. I know I shouldn't. It doesn't seem right after losing Jacob—"

"What if you and Jacob weren't meant to be? Maybe the losses that you and Micah suffered are because *Gott* had a plan to bring you and Micah together."

Katie could only stare at her. "Micah doesn't feel that way about me."

Naomi grinned and gave a nod to someone behind Katie. She turned to find Micah, the man she loved, standing some distance behind her with a smile and a warm look in his bright blue eyes.

"Katie, may I have a minute? There is something I need to tell you."

"Micah," Katie rushed on, hoping that he hadn't overheard her conversation with Naomi.

"Sigh so gude." Please. "It won't take but a minute." His brow furrowed as he waited patiently for her consent.

"Oll recht."

He captured her hand and pulled her gently back toward a cleared area next to the preacher's barn. Once there, he gazed at her without a word.

"Micah, what do you need? If it's to watch your *kinner*, I thought about it and I've changed my mind. I'll be happy to babysit for you."

"Katie," he said huskily, "I don't need you for a babysitter. What I need is you. In my life." He took her other hand so that he was holding both her hands, one in each of his. "I never expected to fall in love again, and I know that you lost someone you loved." His voice broke at the last word. "You're still grieving for..." He looked concerned. "I know what it's like to lose someone. It's hard to move on, but, Katie, I want to move on with you." He paused and gazed at her with love. "I'll wait until you're ready. If you're ever ready." He drew a sharp breath before releasing it. "I hope someday you'll be ready. I love you, Katie."

She gaped at him. "You love me?"

He nodded and she started to laugh, overcome with joy. Stiffening, Micah released her and stepped back. Katie quickly rushed to capture his hands. "You don't have to wait for me to love you, Micah Bontrager," she admitted with a soft smile. "I already do. By allowing me into your life to watch your children, you gave me hope." She softened her gaze as she looked into his eyes—eyes full of love and sudden understanding. "I love you, Micah, so much it hurt when I thought you would be marrying Iris. Then Naomi told me who Iris is to you."

Micah's smile was like bright sunshine after a rainy day. He laughed and pulled her close to him. "I want to marry you, Katie, not because I need a mother for my children. But because I love and need you in my life. Will you be my wife—and a mother to my *kinner*?"

Katie beamed. "*Ja*, Micah! *Ja!* Of course, I will!"

"I want us to marry soon," he said, his features making him more attractive with his happiness on full display. "No long engagements. We can be married this November."

"*Oke.*" She couldn't stop grinning. Katie was eager to tell her parents.

Micah caressed her cheek then took her hand. She was conscious of the warmth of his grip as they walked back to the gathering, holding hands. "I guess Naomi was right. You are my match, Katie. I felt something for you from the first moment she introduced us, but… I was afraid to love again. And I knew you were grieving for… I'm not afraid anymore. You're it for me, Katie." He grinned. "And just so you know, Naomi's match for me was you. It was you who hadn't agreed to marry me yet."

Katie beamed at him. "It was?"

He nodded.

They approached their parents who stood talking in the yard. Her father was clearly ready to leave.

"Mam. Dat," Micah called out.

Both sets of parents turned and saw their son and daughter holding hands.

"Katie?" Mam said, looking hopeful.

"Micah?" Betty gazed at the couple through a film of tears. "Does this mean…"

"*Ja*, Mam. Katie and I are in love and plan to marry as soon as possible."

"Praise the Lord," Micah's and Katie's fathers said with great feeling at the exact same moment. "It's about time."

Katie looked at Micah, and he gazed at her with love—a love that warmed her inside and out. Then they both laughed joyfully.

Their desire to wed was welcomed by their families. It would be a new beginning and a second chance at happiness for them.

Epilogue

Three years later

"Dat, where's Mam?" Jacob asked as he approached his father, who stood, leaning against the kitchen counter, sipping coffee.

Micah eyed his seven-year-old son with affection. "Out in the back hanging clothes." He saw Jacob cast a glance out the window. "What do you need?"

"Should she be doing that?" Jacob looked worried. "Isn't the clothes basket heavy?"

Stifling a smile, Micah nodded as he set down his coffee mug. "*Ja*, but I carried it out for her. Your *endie* Emma would help, but your *mudder* wants to do things herself."

His son looked concerned. "She can't keep working so hard, Dat. Not with the *bubbel* coming."

Micah grew thoughtful. "*Hmm.* I see what you mean." He patted his son on the back. "You and I— we'll just have to help out more." He paused. "Why don't you go outside and see if she needs your assistance."

Jacob bobbed his head. "I'll do that. Where's James?" he asked of his little brother.

"Napping."

"And Eliza and Rebecca?"

"At *Grossmudder* Sarah's."

"Gut." The boy appeared pleased. He put his hands on his hips and rocked back and forth on his heels. "Dat?"

"Ja, soohn?"

"How many more *bruders* and *schweschters* am I going to have?"

Micah started to choke but got himself quickly under control. "As many as *Gott* wants us to have, Jake."

He sighed. *"Oll recht."* He opened the door to head outside then halted to pierce his father with his blue gaze. "You know, Dat, being a big *bruder* can be hard work."

"Ja, I know, *soohn*. I'm a big *bruder."*

Jacob blinked. *"Ja*, that's right!" He grinned as if pleased that he and his father were both big brothers.

The door opened and Micah saw his wife step in, looking lovely in a pale blue maternity dress. "What's going on with *meim* boys?" Katie said as she smiled at Jacob then looked at Micah with eyes filled with love.

"I was coming outside to help you," Jacob said, drawing her attention.

"You were? That was sweet of you," she said. Micah could tell that she hid a smile. He knew his beautiful wife like the back of his hand. She was the love and light of his life. He'd never thought he'd be this happy, and it was all because of Katie Mast Bontrager.

They heard a baby crying from upstairs. Their son James.

"I'll get him," Jacob said.

Micah opened his mouth to object. Katie touched his arm and shook her head, and he relaxed.

"Danki, soohn," Katie said with a smile.

Jacob was big for his age, and Micah knew he was always good with his siblings, patient and kind, a wonderful trait in a big brother. But as a father, he couldn't help worrying about all his children.

Katie gazed at Micah and her heart melted. He looked so handsome in his dark blue shirt that brightened his striking blue eyes. The man held the most special place in her life. She had not expected to be this happy. They hadn't waited long to marry after discovering their love for each other, choosing to wed that November, the month of weddings. It had been a lovely ceremony before their families and the entire church community with Micah's sister Emma and Katie's brother Uri as their attendants.

Micah and she had added to their family a year and a half ago with James. Now they would soon be adding a fifth child. She didn't know if it would be a boy or girl, but it didn't matter. She and Micah simply wanted the baby to be healthy.

Katie thanked the Lord every day for the life she'd been given with her husband and children. "Do you think Jacob and Anna would be happy for us?" she asked Micah as she thought about their first loves.

"*Ja*, I do," Micah replied and flashed her a loving look as he pulled her to his side. "I'd like to think that if they had lived, Anna and I would have moved here to be closer to Mam and Dat. I believe we all would have been close. I think you would have liked Anna and she would have liked you. But—" He stepped back and gazed deeply into her eyes. "I truly believe that *Gott* meant for us to be together. I have never been happier since I took you as my wife."

Eyes glistening with emotion, Katie beamed at him. "And I have never been happier since you became my husband."

They heard footsteps on the stairs. Jacob must be coming down with his baby brother.

"Want to know what Jacob told me before you came inside?" Micah asked with a smile.

Katie shook her head. "He wanted to know how many more children we'd be having. He told me it's a hard job being a big *bruder*."

Delighted, Katie laughed softly. "How precious! I'm surprised, though, because he clearly enjoys his younger siblings."

Micah chuckled. "He does. I think it's his way of discovering how much larger our family will grow."

She reached out and touched her husband's beard, loving the texture of it, loving his features, his temperament and his smile. "Well, *Gott* willing, there will be, at least, one more precious child in our family," she said, rubbing her baby bump. Using her finger, she traced the outline of his mouth when he smiled. "After that, only *Gott* knows the future." She sighed and leaned her head against his chest. "I love you, Micah Bontrager," she breathed.

"I love you, *meim* wife, *meim* heart, *meim* everything."

"Mam, I changed James's diaper before I brought him downstairs," Jacob told them as he carried his baby brother into the room.

"*Gut* job, *soohn*! You're a *wunderbor bruder* and your *mudder*'s special helper," Katie said as she exchanged glances with her husband. The first time Jacob had called her Mam, she'd worried that Micah would be upset, but instead he'd been grinning from ear to ear.

With a nod of approval for Jacob, Micah took James from Jacob's arms and settled him in his high chair. Jacob immediately went into the pantry and returned with a box of the dried cereal that his baby brother was partial to, before he dumped some of the cereal onto James's high chair tray. James instantly began to stuff bits of cereal into his mouth with his little fingers.

With a glimmer of amusement, Micah studied his sons then, eyes twinkling, he caught Katie's gaze. "I love you," he mouthed.

Katie grinned and was filled with warmth and happiness. She never got tired of his confirming his love for her. "I love you, too," she whispered. And she thanked *Gott* every day for the blessings she received and the life she'd been given that fulfilled her like nothing else could.

* * * * *

Dear Reader,

Welcome to the Amish community of New Berne, home to Katie Mast and Micah Bontrager. Katie and Micah's story is a tale of second chances. Devastated by the death of loved ones, neither Katie nor Micah wants to fall in love again. New to the area, Micah, a widower, has no choice but to remarry for the sake of his three motherless young children. He hires a matchmaker to find him a wife. While he can offer a new wife a home, Micah can't—won't—give her his love.

Katie, the Amish matchmaker's first pick for Micah, refuses to wed. When the matchmaker introduces Katie and Micah, Katie sees a man who looks so much like Jacob that she is overcome with grief. Micah is a painful reminder of his younger brother Jacob, Katie's fiancé, who died a month before their wedding. The matchmaker suggests Katie babysits for his three little ones while the search for Micah's new wife continues. Katie agrees, since the situation is temporary. But God has other plans for the couple—and so does a certain Amish matchmaker…

I hope you enjoy this story of forgiveness, hope and love as you live through the trials and tribulations of Micah and Katie who are worthy of happiness and a second chance at love.

I wish you love and peace, and I offer prayers for God's guidance as we each navigate through life.

Blessings and light,
Rebecca Kertz

THE AMISH MATCHMAKING DILEMMA
Amish Country Matches • by Patricia Johns

Amish bachelor Mose Klassen wants a wife who is quiet and traditional—the exact opposite of his childhood friend Naomi Peachy. But when she volunteers as his speech tutor, Mose can't help but be drawn to the outgoing woman. Could an unexpected match be his perfect fit?

TRUSTING HER AMISH HEART
by Cathy Liggett

Leah Zook finds purpose caring for the older injured owner of an Amish horse farm—until his estranged son returns home looking for redemption. The mysterious Zach Graber has all the power to fix the run-down farm—and Leah's locked-down heart. But together will they be strong enough to withstand his secret?

A REASON TO STAY
K-9 Companions • by Deb Kastner

Suddenly responsible for a brother she never knew about, Emma Fitzgerald finds herself out of her depth in a small Colorado town. But when cowboy Sharpe Winslow and his rescue pup, Baloo, take the troubled boy under their wing, Emma can't resist growing close to them and maybe finding a reason to stay...

THE COWGIRL'S REDEMPTION
Hope Crossing • by Mindy Obenhaus

Gloriana Prescott has returned to her Texas ranch to make amends—even if the townsfolk she left behind aren't ready to forgive. But when ranch manager Justin Broussard must save the struggling rodeo, Gloriana sees a chance to prove she's really changed. But can she show Justin, and the town, that she's trustworthy?

FINDING HER VOICE
by Donna Gartshore

Bridget Connelly dreams of buying her boss's veterinary clinic—and so does Sawyer Blume. But it's hard to stay rivals when Sawyer's traumatized daughter bonds with Bridget's adorable pup. When another buyer places a bid, working together might give them everything they want...including each other.

ONCE UPON A FARMHOUSE
by Angie Dicken

Helping her grandmother sell the farm and escaping back to Chicago are all Molly Jansen wants—not to reunite with her ex, single father and current tenant farmer Jack Behrens. But turning Jack and his son out—and not catching feelings for them—might prove more difficult than she realized...

LICNM0722

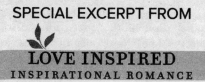
"I'm not easy to match, and I know it," she replied. "My
sister is a matchmaker and even she had trouble with me.
That should tell you something. Maybe it's why I want to
drag some *Englishers* into our midst."

His stomach dropped, and he shot her a look of surprise.

"T-to marry?" he asked.

"No!" Naomi rolled her eyes. "But next to a bunch of
Englishers, I'm downright safe, you know?"

"Yah." He wasn't so fortunate, though. Standing him
next to *Englishers* wouldn't fix what made him different.

"I'm joking, of course. But I do give that impression,
don't I?" Naomi asked with a sigh.

"What?" he asked.

"Of being a rebellious woman, of wanting to jump the
fence," she said. "I don't think I'm actually so different from
the other women—I just don't hide things as well! They're
better at keeping their thoughts to themselves, and mine
come out of my mouth before I think better of them."

"That's…a blessing," he said. At least she was honest.

Naomi put the pitchfork down with a clank of metal against concrete floor. "We're polar opposites, you and me, Mose. I talk too fast, and you aren't able to say everything in your head."

Mose met her gaze. "It's h-hard being d-d-different."

"Amen to that," she murmured. Then she smiled. "But a good friend helps."

Yah, a good friend did help. With Naomi and her wild hair and even wilder way of thinking, he didn't feel so alone—she'd always had that effect on him.

But she was right—Naomi was an example of why the *Ordnung* was so important. Everyone needed to be reined in, given boundaries, made to pause and think. Because if everyone just swung off after their own inclinations, there wouldn't be any Amish community anymore. Everything they valued—the togetherness, the simplicity, the traditions—would be nothing but a memory.

But looking at Naomi, catching her glittering green eyes, he couldn't be the one to hold her back. He could try, but in the end, he wouldn't be able to do it because she'd always been his weakness.

Mose felt his face heat and he wheeled the barrow off toward the door to dump it. She was helping him get more comfortable with talking. That was all. And he'd best remember it.

Don't miss
The Amish Matchmaking Dilemma *by Patricia Johns,*
available September 2022
wherever Love Inspired books and ebooks are sold.

LoveInspired.com

LOVE INSPIRED
INSPIRATIONAL ROMANCE

She could never marry for love.
But what about for a family?

Still grieving her beloved fiancé's death, Katie Mast is not interested in finding a new husband—even if the matchmaker believes widower Micah Bontrager and his three children are perfect for her. But Katie's compassion knows no bounds and she agrees to nanny the little ones. Could this arrangement lead to a life—and love—she thought could never exist again?

CATEGORY: HOPE & INSPIRATION

$6.25 U.S./$7.25 CAN.

ISBN-13: 978-1-335-58512-7

50625

9 781335 585127

EAN

S

Uplifting stories of faith, forgiveness and hope.

LOVE INSPIRED
LoveInspired.com